"Let's go, but stay to my left, okay?"

They left the motel, keeping close to the building as they rounded the corner to the back.

Kari didn't say much once she was safe inside his car, and he drove away from the motel, although he could tell she was watching the road behind them for any sign of the SUV that had shot at them. He hated knowing she was so afraid.

He headed for the interstate, but they were on the freeway for barely ten minutes when bright headlights gained on them from behind. Marc tensed when he realized the vehicle was an SUV.

The same one as before? How was that possible?

He hit the gas, determined to put distance between them.

"Gun!" Kari shouted. Sure enough, he could see the narrow barrel of a gun poking through the passenger-side window just like it had earlier.

"Hang on," he said, pushing the speed limit as much as he dared.

"Not again! Please, not again!"

Kari's desperate cry stabbed like a hot poker in his gut. He'd promised to keep her safe.

He couldn't bear the thought of failure. Of losing another witness.

A pregnant witness.

Laura Scott is a nurse by day and an author by night. She has always loved romance, reading faith-based books by Grace Livingston Hill in her teenage years. She's thrilled to have published sixteen books for Love Inspired Suspense. She has two adult children and lives in Milwaukee, Wisconsin, with her husband of thirty years. Please visit Laura at laurascottbooks.com, as she loves to hear from her readers.

Books by Laura Scott

Love Inspired Suspense

Callahan Confidential

Shielding His Christmas Witness

SWAT: Top Cops

Wrongly Accused
Down to the Wire
Under the Lawman's Protection
Forgotten Memories
Holiday on the Run
Mirror Image

Visit the Author Profile page at Harlequin.com for more titles.

SHIELDING HIS CHRISTMAS WITNESS

LAURA SCOTT

HARLEQUIN® LOVE INSPIRED® SUSPENSE

Recycling programs
for this product may
not exist in your area.

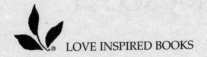 LOVE INSPIRED BOOKS

ISBN-13: 978-0-373-67786-3

Shielding His Christmas Witness

Copyright © 2016 by Laura Iding

www.Harlequin.com

Printed in U.S.A.

All the prophets testify about him, that everyone who believes in him receives forgiveness of sins through his name.
—*Acts* 10:43

This book is dedicated to my cousin Carol Goodfellow. Carol, thanks for always being supportive of me and my books. Love you!

ONE

A muffled thud startled Kari Danville, pulling her out of a sound sleep. She froze, heart racing as she blinked in the darkness, straining to listen.

Silence.

She placed a protective hand over her slightly rounded abdomen, trying to tell herself she and her baby were safe. The noise she'd heard was not someone trying to get inside the safe house. It was only her imagination going into overdrive.

Special Agent Marc Callahan promised no one other than the bank-robbery task force members knew she'd been moved here. And there was an officer stationed right outside. Kari forced herself to take a deep breath, letting it out slowly. No reason to think the serial bank robber she was now scheduled to testify against in a week's time had sent his buddies after her.

The sound of shattering glass made a mockery of her attempt to remain calm. Kari reacted instinctively, leaping out of bed and grabbing her phone as she quickly shoved her feet into running shoes.

She had to get out of here. Now!

Thankfully, she'd been sleeping in a pair of thick stretch pants and a long-sleeved T-shirt. Yanking a sweatshirt over her head wasted a precious moment, but then she quickly made her way over to the window. The sash lifted easily enough, but removing the storm window was difficult. Willing her fingers not to shake, she finally managed to pry the window out of the frame.

She threw her leg over the sill. At eighteen weeks along, she was still fairly flexible, but she couldn't help worrying the short drop would somehow harm her baby. Halfway out the window, she heard the bedroom door bang open.

No!

She tumbled to the ground at the same time she heard two muffled bangs. Something whizzed past her head.

He was shooting at her!

Her ankle twisted as she landed hard, but she ignored the throbbing pain as she sprinted through the cold winter night, crossing the snow-covered ground in order to reach the protective shadows of the evergreen trees behind the safe house.

Lord, keep me and my baby safe in Your care!

The prayer helped her to remain calm. Where should she go? She needed to call for help, either Detective Monique Barclay or FBI agent Marc Callahan, but didn't dare stop long enough to use her phone. She had to assume the gunman had followed her footprints in the snow to the small wooded area. From there, the bare areas on the ground around the trees helped hide her trail.

What if the intruder wasn't alone? Her chest squeezed with fear at the thought of others being somewhere outside, lying in wait for her.

She reached the shelter of a cluster of trees along the edge of the property, but kept going, stepping carefully to avoid leaving footprints. Her breath created puffs of condensation that she feared the gunman might be able to see, so she lifted the edge of her sweatshirt to cover her mouth.

The house where she'd been staying was located at a quiet and secluded dead-end street. Hugging the shadows, she made her way around to the front of the house. There was a policeman sitting in a squad car outside the house. If she could get to him, he'd be able to drive them to safety and call for backup.

Kari took cover behind a huge oak tree, pausing for a moment to catch her breath. From her position she could see the police car parked beside the curb. She frowned, the tiny hairs on the back of her neck rising in alarm. The vehicle looked empty, no shadow indicating a person was seated behind the wheel. No sign of condensation on the windows, either. Where was Officer Wallace? Was he outside making rounds?

Or had something happened to him?

Kari swallowed hard and stepped softly through the brush, going from one tree to the next in a direction far from the so-called safe house. She needed to keep moving. To get as far away from the gunman as possible.

She stumbled and fell to her knees. The cold, wet snow made damp patches on her pants. A sob rose in the back of her throat, but she relentlessly pushed herself upright, wiping her snowy hands on her hips. She swept her gaze over the area, searching for someplace to hide.

The sound of a branch snapping in half echoed through the night, spurring her into action. There was a shed up ahead, but that hiding spot was too obvious. She needed something better.

But what?

She crossed several more backyards in a zigzag pattern, choosing those that were already trampled with kid-sized footprints. She lost track of how many blocks she'd passed when she saw it. A long rope ladder dangling from a thick tree branch. Tipping her head back, she noticed there was a small tree house made out of mismatched wood, nestled in the branches.

Without giving herself time to change her mind, she grabbed the rope and quickly ascended the swaying ladder to the platform of the tree house. Once she was safely inside, she pulled up the ladder behind her, hoping and praying that if the assailant went past, he wouldn't notice.

The interior of the structure was dark, the gaps in the wood frame letting in the frigid air along with a tiny sliver of moonlight. For the first time since waking up to the sound of an intruder, she felt a modicum of safety. Kari pulled out the disposable phone she'd been given and quickly searched for the emergency contact information she'd been provided. Agent Callahan's number came up and she quickly placed the call.

"Callahan," he answered gruffly on the second ring.

She nearly wept in relief. "It's me, Kari Danville," she whispered. "I need your help. Someone found me and tried to kill me."

"What?" Agent Callahan's harsh voice made her wince. From the moment they'd met, there was something about his stern demeanor that put her on edge. Oh, he was handsome enough, tall with dark hair and strikingly green eyes. His broad shoulders gave her the impression he worked out a lot, too. But she'd found it difficult to warm up to a man who never smiled.

"Where's the officer guarding your house?" he demanded.

"I don't know," she admitted. "The squad car is still out there, but I didn't see anyone inside."

"Where are you?" he asked. She could hear rustling sounds as he moved around.

"Hiding in a tree house," she whispered.

There was a long pause. "A tree house?" he echoed in surprise. "Where?"

"I'm not sure. I went through several neighbors' yards to get away."

More background noises. "Stay where you are, understand? Don't contact anyone else. Wait for me… I'll be there as soon as possible."

"Okay." She didn't want to disconnect from the call, wanting, needing human contact. But she forced herself to push the end button before sliding the phone back into the pocket of her hooded sweatshirt.

She shivered and once again placed a protective hand over her belly. "We're going to be all right," she promised her unborn baby. "God is watching over us. He'll make sure Agent Callahan finds us and takes us someplace safe."

Kari closed her eyes, struggling to hold on to the thin thread of hope.

Truthfully, her life had fallen apart shortly

before the bank robbery. Discovering that her fiancé had suddenly vanished had been difficult enough, but then she found out Vince had also cleaned out their joint bank account, taking every last dime they'd been saving for their wedding. Angry and destitute, she'd taken her modest engagement ring to a jeweler, only to be told it was fake and completely worthless.

Finding out she was pregnant was an even bigger shock, but after the first wave of hopelessness had washed over her, she'd decided to treat this baby as a blessing. Yes, the baby's father had abandoned her, but obviously she was better off without Vince Ackerman. She still had her job at the bank, and her boss had been kind enough to grant her a leave of absence in order to testify at trial. When this mess was over, she would be able to provide a loving home for her baby.

The same way her mother had raised her.

Kari huddled in the corner of the tree house, wondering if it was time to tell Agent Callahan she was expecting. Not that her condition mattered to him one way or the other; all he needed was for her to testify at trial. A trial that had been moved up to the first week of December after her name was leaked to the press.

If only she hadn't gotten such a good look at the bank robber's yellow-gold eyes and intricate chest tattoo. If only she wasn't a graphic artist, noticing every detail of the tattoo to the point she'd been able to draw an exact replica of the complicated design. Of course it was Terrance Jamison's fault that he shot and killed a bank patron, increasing the charges against him.

She hadn't known until Agent Callahan showed up later that day that any bank robbery was a federal crime. Or that Jamison and his cohorts were believed to be responsible for almost a dozen heists that took place in a two week time frame. The robbers had hit hard and fast, sending them soaring to the top of the Milwaukee FBI's most wanted list.

The FBI had only one of the bank robbers, Terrance Jamison, in custody, but the Feds and local police suspected there were at least two others involved, maybe more.

But Jamison wasn't talking.

Knowing that his friends had found her location at the safe house made her both upset and angry. It wasn't just her life at stake. She desperately needed Agent Callahan to do a better job of protecting her.

For her sake as well as her baby's.

FBI agent Marc Callahan jammed his key into the ignition, hardly able to comprehend that the location of the safe house had been breached.

First Kari's name had been leaked to the press,

now this. Only a few people knew where he'd stashed her. His key witness should have been safe.

Punching the gas, he shot out of his underground parking garage and up onto the street, anxious to reach the safe house as soon as possible. Had Kari Danville imagined someone breaking in? Trying to kill her?

No. To be fair, she didn't seem the type to give in to hysterics. When he'd watched the tape of the bank robbery, he'd been impressed by her cool head and logical thinking. The way her artist's eye had picked up every intricate detail of Jamison's chest tattoo had been an added bonus, making her a very credible witness. The fact that she'd gotten a glimpse of the tattoo at all had been a freak accident—one of the bank patrons had foolishly decided to rush at Jamison during the robbery. Jamison fought him off, but the customer had grabbed on to his hoodie, dragging it to the side enough to reveal the tattoo. Of course Jamison shot the bystander, killing him. Despite the customer's efforts, Jamison had managed to get away with a significant amount of money.

Fortunately, they'd been able to apprehend Jamison shortly afterward, thanks to Kari's drawing of the tattoo. A sharp patrol officer had pulled Jamison over on a routine traffic stop. At the time he was no longer wearing the hoodie, just a tank top, which enabled the officer to recognize a portion of the tattoo and to arrest Jamison. Unfortunately, the perp wasn't talking, so they didn't have any leads on his accomplices.

Time was running out, since Jamison's attorney had convinced the judge to expedite the trial.

Which brought him back to the present situation. How had Kari been found? A mistake on her part? Or a leak from inside?

And how was it that the press had gotten her name? A fluke...or was it something more sinister? Too many questions, not nearly enough answers.

He clenched his jaw so hard it ached. No way was he going to lose another witness.

Not this time. Not on his watch.

Marc pulled up in front of the safe house and parked behind the squad car. The area looked deserted, but he approached carefully, his gun drawn as he peered inside the vehicle. The officer was slumped against the center console, halfway lying on the passenger-side seat, clearly dead.

He scowled, his gut clenching at the needless loss of life and swept another gaze over the area. Kari Danville hadn't been exaggerating after all. She'd been smart enough to get away. Hiding in a tree house no less.

Spinning around, he headed back to his car.

There was no point in going through the house; his main priority right now was to find his witness.

After executing a tight U-turn, Marc reached for his phone and called Kari.

"Hello?" Her voice was a thready whisper of sound.

"I'm on my way, but I need your help. Can you see any landmarks? Something to clue me in as to where to find you?"

"Give me a minute." The phone went silent for an incredibly long moment. He drove down the street located east of the safe house, searching for any sign of a tree house. "The tree house is in the backyard but I can see there are two houses on either side of me. One is a Cape Cod with white siding and black trim. The other is a ranch home in dark brown. I think the ranch has Christmas lights out front—I can see a red and green glow."

"That's good," he said encouragingly. "What about the house where the tree house is located? What can you tell me about that?"

"The angle makes it hard to see. Almost as if the tree house was built in a way to hide the occupants from being seen from the house. It's small, but I can't quite make out the color. Maybe white, or something light. The roof is dark. That's all I can tell you."

Great. If the tree house was located in the backyard, then he wouldn't be able to see it from the street.

Not necessarily a bad thing, since no one else could see it from the road, either.

"Agent Callahan?" Her soft voice dragged him from his thoughts.

"Yes?"

"Should I climb down to meet you someplace?"

"No, stay where you are. Don't worry, I'll find you." The last thing he wanted was for her to leave the sanctuary of the tree house. He was surprised she'd even suggested it, especially since the temperature outside was below freezing. Hopefully, the structure would provide her some shelter from the wind. He couldn't help admiring Kari's strength and determination. "I'll call again when I find the two houses you mentioned."

"Okay, thanks."

The phone went dead and he had the insane urge to call her back, to keep her on the line. Which was ridiculous since he needed to concentrate on finding the Cape Cod and ranch home she'd identified. Blazing Christmas lights were an added bonus.

Driving up one street and down the next had stretched his patience to the limit, when he abruptly found them. She'd been right about the Christmas decorations; the brown ranch had red and green spotlights outside shining on the birch trees in the front yard. On the other side was the white Cape Cod she'd mentioned. And nestled between them, a small house with either gray or light blue siding.

Marc pulled over to the side of the road and threw the gearshift into Park. Kari had run farther than she'd realized, since this place was a good ten blocks from the safe house. He glanced around, making sure no one else was lurking nearby.

The area seemed quiet, peaceful and deserted, not entirely surprising considering it was nearly three o'clock in the morning.

He grabbed his phone then slipped from the car, closing the door as quietly as possible behind him. He walked up the driveway of the white Cape Cod, before making his way across the snow to the backyard of the grayish-blue house.

There was a huge tree located dead center of the grassy area. It wasn't until he was directly underneath it that he could make out the roughly constructed tree house.

How on earth had Kari noticed it?

He called her phone, smiling grimly when he

could hear a low buzz from up above. Smart girl, she had her phone on vibrate.

"Agent Callahan?"

"I found your tree house," he said in a hushed tone. "How did you get up there, anyway?"

"There's a rope ladder. Stay back. I'll climb down."

He disconnected from the call, slipping his phone in his back pocket. When the rope ladder appeared through a square opening in the base of the tree house, he waited until it hit the ground before grabbing it with both hands and holding it steady. He felt the tension on the rope when she began climbing.

When she was close enough, he stepped back, giving her room to maneuver. She stepped off the ladder, then stumbled sideways as her legs gave out.

Marc instinctively reached out to catch her in his arms. "Easy, you're safe now."

Her entire body shook; her fingers curled into his black leather jacket as if holding on for dear life. "I know. But I twisted my ankle climbing out the window," she confessed.

He tightened his grip on her slender frame, biting back a flash of frustration intermixed with anger. This poor woman shouldn't have had to climb out a window and then run for her life in the snow and cold. Of course, a good cop shouldn't have been shot, either.

None of this boded well for the upcoming trial.

She let out a squeak of surprise when he swept her into his arms. "What are you doing?" she asked, her arms clamping tightly around his neck.

Ignoring the obvious, he swiftly retraced his previous route between the two houses, carrying her to the street. When he reached his car, he gently set her down, waiting until she was steady before releasing her.

"I could have walked," she protested, leaning against the vehicle in a way that took weight off her left leg.

He shrugged and opened the passenger-side door. "Walking on a bad sprain delays healing," he muttered, wondering who he was trying to convince. Once she was safely inside the car, he shut the door and then jogged around to the driver's side.

For some odd reason her cranberry-vanilla scent seemed to cling to his clothing. He gave himself a mental head-smack to snap himself back to reality.

He hadn't been this acutely aware of a woman in a long time. A full two years had passed since his wife's death in a terrible car crash. He'd locked his emotions away in a deep freeze; no reason for the ice in his heart to melt now.

Kari Danville might be pretty with her chocolate-brown hair and deep brown eyes, but she was also his witness. Once the trial was over and she was relocated with a new identity, he'd never see her again.

A fact that suited him just fine.

"Where are we going?" Kari asked, breaking the strained silence between them.

He cleared his throat. "Somewhere safe."

She scowled and crossed her arms defensively across her chest. "Yeah, that was what you said two days ago."

Knowing she was right didn't make things easier. "I know."

"I don't understand. How did they find me?" she demanded. "I thought no one knew where I was staying?"

The same question had been badgering him since the moment he'd answered her call. And he hated to admit the implication of the night's events was staggering. "If you haven't called anyone—"

"I haven't!"

"—then there must be a leak somewhere."

Her mouth opened, shut and then opened again. "What department? The police? The FBI?"

"I'm not sure," he admitted, trying to hide the

weariness in his voice. "The bank-robbery task force has both Milwaukee Police detectives and FBI agents involved. Either way, I intend to get to the bottom of this."

"It doesn't make sense," she murmured. "No logical reason that anyone working within law enforcement would attempt to protect a bank robber."

He was inclined to agree. "You're right, but I don't have any other explanation. Do you?"

"No." She turned away, staring out the window in a way that made him frown. Had he imagined the flash of guilt in her eyes? Was she hiding something?

Trust didn't come easily, especially when it came to women. His wife's secret had killed her, leaving him reeling from the extent of her lies.

"Kari, tell me the truth. Did you call anyone other than me?" he asked.

"No, I didn't. Check my phone if you want." She pulled out the disposable cell he'd given her and dropped it in the cup holder between them.

Marc picked up the phone and tucked it in his pocket. He could check her calls, but he doubted they'd found her via a throw-away phone.

No, it was more likely that one of the officers involved in protecting her had leaked the safe-house location. On purpose? By accident?

"Maybe they traced me through your phone

calls," she said in a frost-tinged voice. "I might be better off alone."

He couldn't argue her logic about the possible trace on his calls, especially if the leak was someone within the task force. But abandoning her was out of the question. "You're not better off alone. For one thing…you need to testify in court, or all of this would be for nothing. Remember, an innocent man has died because of Jamison."

She sighed, but didn't say anything.

"I promise you're safe with me. And you're right, I have no way of knowing where the leak is coming from." He opened his window and tossed out his work cell phone, wincing a bit when it shattered on the asphalt. Then he tossed out her disposable phone, as well.

"I—I can't believe you did that," she gasped in surprise.

"Yeah, well, I promised to keep you safe, didn't I?" He headed for the nearest on-ramp, intending to take the interstate in a northwest direction. He needed to find a motel, preferably off the beaten track.

"Yes, you did," she murmured in a subdued voice.

They drove in silence for a good ten minutes. He kept his eyes peeled for an appropriate place to stop for what was left of the night.

"Agent Callahan?"

"Call me Marc," he suggested gruffly. No reason to stand on formality, not when they were going to be spending the next five days together.

"I— There's something I need to tell you."

His gut tightened with apprehension. Had Kari done something that caused the leak after all? "What?"

She twisted her fingers in her lap, clearly nervous. "I'm pregnant."

"Excuse me?" He shook his head, certain he hadn't heard her correctly.

"I'm pregnant," she repeated. "I'm due in about six months."

Whatever he'd expected her to say, this wasn't it. He struggled to pull his scattered thoughts into some semblance of order. "Why didn't you say something sooner?"

"My personal life wasn't any of your business. But now I need you to understand how important it is for me to be safe. Plus, I had to leave my prenatal vitamins behind, so we'll need to stop at a drugstore so I can pick up another bottle."

Pregnant? Vitamins?

The knowledge that Kari was expecting shouldn't affect him like this, but somehow the nightmare of his past collided with the present.

No one knew the truth about his wife. How Jessica had been pregnant when she'd died.

Or the fact that DNA testing had proven he wasn't the baby's father.

He shook off the overwhelming sense of failure with effort. Jessica's lies didn't matter right now. He needed to focus on the situation at hand.

He gripped the steering wheel tightly. A dead cop and a breached safe house. Things couldn't get much worse than that. He needed to get control of this situation and fast.

Before any more innocent people were placed in harm's way.

TWO

A thick, heavy silence stretched between them, to the point Kari felt as if she might suffocate. Tension radiated off Marc's body in waves, battering her already-frayed nerves.

She didn't know what he was thinking. Was he upset with her for some reason? And if so, why? She was the one who'd been forced to run from a madman shooting at her. She was the one who'd almost been killed.

Her baby that had been placed in danger.

Five minutes passed, then ten. Finally, she couldn't stand it a moment longer. "What is your problem? Why are you mad at me?"

He relaxed his grip on the steering wheel, glancing over at her in surprise. "I'm not."

"Really? Then why are you scowling?"

He grimaced. "Because a good cop died tonight and someone almost killed you. Isn't that enough of a reason to be angry?"

"I guess." She turned to stare blindly out the

passenger-side window, wondering when Agent Callahan, er—Marc—would find a place to stop. The aftermath of adrenaline left her feeling shaky and weak. Exhausted.

Of course her fatigue could just as easily be related to her condition.

He fell silent again, maybe brooding about the case. A few minutes later, he exited the freeway. He waited for the light to turn green before heading down to a parking lot located in front of a small single-story motel. No fancy names here, just Ravenswood Motel located in the nondescript and unincorporated town of Ravenswood.

When he pulled up in front of the lobby, he turned off the car and took the keys out of the ignition. "I need you to wait here."

She sighed. "Not like I have much choice considering my ankle is swollen and hurts like crazy."

He barely looked at her. "If it's just a sprain, I'd rather not risk taking you to an emergency department."

Yeah, she wasn't really keen on that idea, either. "I'm sure I'll be fine."

He gave a terse nod, then pushed open his door and slid out from behind the wheel. The moment he disappeared inside, she was nearly overwhelmed by a wave of loneliness.

Ridiculous, because she wasn't alone. Marc

was here with her. But the sense of camaraderie she'd experienced earlier seemed to have vanished.

Where was the nice, chivalrous guy who'd carried her to the car so she wouldn't have to walk on her bum ankle? The man who'd tossed out his own cell phone as a way to keep her safe?

She blew out a breath, realizing that his changed attitude was likely because she was pregnant and not married. From the moment she'd discovered she was expecting, she'd run into some of the same judgmental sneers, especially from the older generation.

Not that she was proud of the fact she'd given in to temptation. At the time she'd justified her actions by the fact that she and Vince were engaged to be married in a few short months. They were in love, or so she'd thought.

Until he'd disappeared without a trace, leaving her high and dry. And pregnant.

Shame tasted bitter on her tongue, but she refused to let it get to her. Her baby was a precious gift, one she was determined to cherish, no matter what.

Ironically, the place she'd found solace and acceptance had been in her friend Amy's church. The people there had been wonderful, including the pastor. Someday, soon, she'd have her baby baptized there.

Something to look forward to.

The thought of raising her baby alone was both thrilling and terrifying. She wished her mother were still alive to offer some advice. Especially since her own father, much like Vince, had disappeared, leaving her mother and her to survive on their own.

Despite being abandoned, her mother had always maintained a sunny outlook on life, while providing a loving, stable home environment for Kari. Not that things had been easy, because they hadn't. Still, she couldn't complain. In fact, she hoped and prayed she'd find a way to do the same with her own baby.

Marc returned to the car, interrupting her thoughts with his intimidating presence, even as he wordlessly slid behind the wheel. He drove the short distance to park in front of room number seven. He climbed out again, then came around to open her passenger-side door. "Ready?"

"Of course." She summoned the strength to swing her legs around, wincing when she placed pressure on her left ankle. Marc surprised her by holding out his arm. "Lean on me."

The radiating pain shooting through her foot didn't give her much choice. She braced herself on his arm and hobbled the few steps it took to reach the door. Then she rested against the wall of the building, waiting for him to use the motel key card to open the door.

He held out his hand again, so she leaned against him, making her way inside. By the time she collapsed on the bed, her ankle felt as if it might explode. She closed her eyes, fighting a sense of helplessness.

Not being able to walk made her dependent on Marc for more than just keeping her safe.

Her eyelids sprang open in surprise when he lifted her swollen ankle up off the mattress. "What are you doing?"

"You need to keep this elevated on pillows," he said calmly, untying her shoe and stuffing two pillows beneath her calf and heel. He gently probed the skin around her ankle, emitting a low whistle from under his breath. "This looks worse than I expected."

She wasn't sure what to say to that. He disappeared into the bathroom, ran water and then returned with an icy cold towel, which he wrapped tightly around her ankle. She had to admit the coolness against her swollen joint offered a bit of relief.

"I'll get some ice." He grabbed the plastic bucket off the small table and disappeared again, the door of the motel room closing loudly behind him.

She let out her pent-up breath in a heavy sigh.

Was it normal for FBI agents to blow hot and cold so quickly? One minute he's scowling and brooding, the next he's fetching ice for her ankle.

Men. Who could figure them out? Vince had already fooled her once; she refused to be gullible again.

She placed a protective hand over her abdomen. She'd dreamed of having a large family, a future Vince had conned her into believing he wanted, as well. Unfortunately, it wasn't meant to be.

She was facing her future, alone.

Please, Lord, give me strength.

The door opened a few minutes later and Marc walked in, bringing the familiar sandalwood scent with him. She didn't want to be so aware of him, but she was. He wrapped some crushed ice in a towel and then pressed it against her ankle.

"Thanks," she murmured.

He pulled up a chair and sat down beside her. "We need to talk."

What she really needed was sleep, but she turned her head to look at him. "Okay."

"Where's your baby's father?"

Huh? She frowned, wondering why it mattered. "I have no clue. I haven't seen him in a long time."

His green eyes were skeptical. "Are you sure?

He's probably worried about you. Give me his name and contact information. I'll find a way to keep him informed."

She stifled a sigh. "Vince left me three months ago. He doesn't even know I'm pregnant."

He lifted a surprised brow. "Really?"

"Yeah."

"Okay, Vince what?" Marc picked up the motel pen and notepad.

"Ackerman. Vince Ackerman." She rattled off the last phone number she had for him. "You can try to call, but trust me, the line has been disconnected. I honestly don't have any idea where he is."

"I believe you." His tone was considerate, but that didn't stop him from writing Vince's name and number on the sheet of paper. "Did Detective Monique Barclay do a background check on him?"

She shrugged. "I have no idea." She wasn't sure why anyone cared about Vince. It wasn't as if he was involved in the bank robberies.

"Try to get some rest, okay?"

"Sure." Easier said than done with the way her ankle throbbed.

"I'll be in the connecting room right next door." He rose to his feet, then hesitated, staring at the motel phone that sat on the bedside table beside her.

Her stomach clenched. Was it possible that he still didn't trust her? She half expected him to disconnect the phone from the wall, but then he walked past the device toward the connecting door between their rooms. "I'm going to leave this open an inch or so. Just give a yell if you need anything."

She nodded. "Good night."

"Good night." Marc disappeared into his own room, leaving her to stare helplessly at the four walls surrounding her. She fought the urge to call him back.

Maybe she trusted him to keep her and her baby safe, but she couldn't afford to allow herself to depend on anyone but herself.

Hadn't Vince already taught her not to trust her instincts? Bad enough that she'd been foolish enough to fall for his act.

Tears pricked at her eyelids, evidence of hormones running amuck.

Five days. She needed to remain strong for the next five days. Once the trial was over, things would get back to normal.

Whatever her new normal might be.

Doing his best to keep quiet so he wouldn't disturb Kari, Marc pulled his laptop computer out of its carrying case and set it on the small table. His witness deserved her rest, especially considering the condition of her ankle.

He wished there was more he could do for her, but it was better for him to focus on the case.

He'd gone through the bank-robbery case file more than once, but didn't remember seeing anything about a former boyfriend named Vince Ackerman. Even if Detective Barclay had cleared the guy, shouldn't she have at least mentioned Vince in the report?

Marc also needed to try to figure out who could have possibly leaked the location of the safe house. He doubted Kari had done anything on purpose, but he couldn't ignore the tiny voice in his head telling him she might have let something slip by accident.

Maybe at the drugstore? When buying her prenatal vitamins? Or had she been followed?

He could almost hear his sister Madison's voice in his head, admonishing him for being so cynical. And maybe he was. Not just because of his line of work, but learning the truth about Jessica and then losing the witness in his last case. A case that was eerily similar to this one. A young man from last year, who'd also witnessed a bank robbery.

Only Joey Simmons had been shot and killed on the way to the courthouse the morning of the trial, rather than a week before. They'd eventually proven that the man their star witness had been about to testify against had hired the gunman to kill Simmons. To this day, Marc felt guilty about that. As if he should have known or done something to avoid the outcome.

Was it any wonder he didn't trust anyone?

His sister, Maddy, was a prosecuting attorney in the DA's office, working hard to bring perpetrators to justice. She met all sorts of low-life criminals, yet still managed to maintain a positive outlook on life.

How she managed that feat was beyond his comprehension.

He booted up the computer, then drummed his fingers on the table as he waited for the operating system to kick in. As soon as the wallpaper image bloomed on his screen, he opened a browser and began a background search on Vince Ackerman.

He found several, but none in the right age range. Or what he thought was the correct age range. Somehow he couldn't picture Kari with a guy fifteen years her senior.

Although what did he really know about her? Other than the basics?

Kari Ann Danville was twenty-six years old, grew up in Oakdale, Wisconsin, a suburb just outside Milwaukee. She'd been working at the Oakdale National Bank for the past four years, since graduating from college with an associate's degree in graphic arts.

Graphic arts and banking didn't necessarily go hand in hand, but he'd also found a freelance graphic-arts website hosted by KariAnn's Designs. Maybe she was using the regular paychecks from her day job at the bank while she worked on getting her design business off the ground.

He wondered what she'd do once the baby was born. Not that Kari's life or career prospects were any of his business. He couldn't afford to let the aching loneliness in her eyes get to him.

Which brought him back to the baby's father, Vince Ackerman. He scowled at the federal database he was logged in to. There were a few possibilities, but all of them were located on the other side of the country.

He sat back with a sigh. He should have asked for the guy's age, and his last known address, but couldn't bring himself to go next door to wake her up.

Marc scrubbed his hands over his face, knowing he should follow her lead and get some sleep, too. But he needed to figure out his next steps, not least of which involved contacting his boss.

The dead cop and empty safe house would raise an alarm when the relief officer arrived on the scene, in roughly—he glanced at his watch—

two-and-a-half hours. His boss, Special Agent in Charge Evan White, would demand answers.

Unfortunately, he didn't have any.

Since he'd ditched his phone, he had to use the motel phone. He reluctantly lifted the handset of the motel phone and dialed the main office number. No one would answer, but he could use a passcode to access Evan's mailbox.

"This is Callahan reporting in," he said into the voice mail. "I have our witness in custody, but the safe house was breached and the officer watching over her is dead, the result of a gunshot wound inflicted at close range. I don't have my phone... I'll let you know as soon as I secure a replacement."

He disconnected from the call, relieved to postpone the inevitable confrontation with his boss.

They were safely isolated here for the moment, but they couldn't just hang out here until the trial. He needed help from someone he could trust.

His family.

As the oldest, he didn't like turning to his siblings for help. His brother Miles was the next in line, and also happened to be a detective with the Milwaukee Police Department. There were six Callahans total, and thanks to his parents' crazy sense of humor all their names started with the letter M.

Marcus, Miles, Mitch, Michael, Matthew and Madison. Matt and Maddy were twins, Matt the elder by three minutes. Maddy hated being the baby of the family, constantly lamenting the fact that she had five older brothers. His father had been thrilled to finally have a daughter, and while they were always protective of their baby sister, they'd all also spoiled Maddy a little too much.

He swallowed the painful lump in his throat when he thought about their father. Max Callahan had been a cop, and the acting chief of police, before he was killed six months ago, in the line of duty.

His mother, Maggie, and their grandmother, Nan, still lived in the house where they grew up. Sunday church service followed by brunch was a steadfast Callahan tradition.

Max Callahan had instilled a strong sense of duty and commitment to serving their community in all of his children. And the Callahan legacy lived on, as they'd followed in his footsteps in one form or another, well, except for Michael, who worked as a private investigator. Their father hadn't been thrilled with Mike's choice and had constantly badgered him to go back to the police academy.

It still burned Marc to know their father's case remained unsolved. Especially since his father was murdered by a sniper during an investigation into a police shooting of an unarmed teenager. It wasn't normal for the chief of police to go to crime scenes, but his dad had wanted to make a statement that they were taking these types of incidents seriously.

Only to be shot and killed for his efforts.

Marc had recently begun his own personal investigation into his father's death, hating the thought that the person responsible might get away with the crime. But it was as if the shooter had vanished into thin air, without leaving so much as a shell casing behind as a clue to his, or her, identity.

Marc must be more tired than he thought, to allow his thoughts to be sucked back into the past.

Unfortunately, he couldn't allow his father's death to become a distraction.

Not when faced with an immediate threat to his witness.

He picked up the motel phone again and punched in his brother's number. Several rings went by before Miles answered in a raspy voice.

"Who is this?"

"Marc. I need a favor."

As if by magic the sleepiness in his brother's

voice vanished. "What's going on? Why are you calling me from an unknown number?"

"That's the favor," he said, avoiding a direct answer. "I need two new untraceable phones. Are you in the middle of something? Can you get them to me ASAP?"

"That depends on where you are," Miles said. "Is this related to your serial bank-robbery case?"

"Yeah. The safe house where I stashed my witness has been compromised. I don't want to call the Feds or the locals for help. Not until I have a better understanding as to what's going on."

Miles was quiet for a long moment. "That's not good," he finally said. "Okay. Prepaid phones, check. Anything else?"

He knew his brother would come through for him. "Not at the moment, but I'll let you know if that changes."

"Where are you?"

"Ravenswood Motel. It's off Highway WW— on the right. You can't miss it."

"Okay, but it will take me some time to get there and I have to wait for the stores to open."

"Understood. Thanks, I owe you."

"Yeah, and don't think I won't collect," Miles shot back. "Later, bro."

Marc hung up the phone then glanced up in

time to see Kari standing in the opening between the connecting doors. He was surprised to see her up and moving around on her injured ankle.

"Who was that?" she demanded.

"My brother." Marc slowly rose to his feet. "How's the ankle?"

"Don't try to change the subject," she said, narrowing her gaze. "Why are you calling your family? I thought we were supposed to stay off the grid."

"We are. Relax. My brother would never betray me."

"That doesn't necessarily make *me* feel better."

The edge of desperation in her tone made him frown. "You're my witness," he pointed out. "Of course Miles would protect you, too."

"Really? I'm not so sure." Sarcasm didn't seem to be her style, but she appeared to be on a roll. "First Vince disappears without a trace, taking every cent out of our joint account, then I get robbed while working at the bank, and then end up running away from a gunman..."

Whoa, wait a minute. He backtracked a bit. "Vince stole money from you?"

Her eyes widened as if realizing what she'd said. With an awkward turn while leaning heavily on the wall, she disappeared inside her room, shutting and locking the connecting door behind her with a loud click.

Marc stared at the closed door, his thoughts whirling. Maybe the reason he hadn't been able to find Vince Ackerman was because the guy didn't really exist. His name, his entire identity, was likely fake.

A chill snaked down his spine.

Was Vince just another con man, out to score off naive women? Or was it possible Vince was involved in something more sinister?

THREE

Bracing her arm against the wall, Kari hopped on one foot over to the bed. When she'd gotten up earlier to use the bathroom, she'd heard voices. Seeing Marc on the phone had made her see red.

Now that the initial flash of anger had passed, she could admit that she'd overreacted. It was probably better that he'd called his brother, rather than anyone within the police department or FBI. He was right about one thing—his brother would likely do whatever was necessary to help them out.

If only she'd managed to control her temper. The slip she'd made revealing how Vince had taken all their money, most of which had been hers, anyway, hadn't gone unnoticed.

Then again, she doubted that there was much that passed by Agent Marc Callahan. For some odd reason, knowing he had family, at least one brother, made him seem more human.

Plopping back down on the bed, she lifted her injured ankle and set it gently on the pillows. The ice inside the towel had melted, but she wasn't in the mood to ask Marc for more.

Later, she'd find the energy to get up and get more ice herself.

There was nothing worse than feeling helpless, than being at someone else's mercy. But that was the situation she was in, at least for now.

She managed to fall asleep, despite the throbbing in her ankle. The next time she opened her eyes, the sun was shining brightly through the narrow opening between the curtains hanging over the window. Gingerly taking her leg off the pillows, she rolled onto her side and sat up, pushing her dark hair away from her face.

Gathering every ounce of strength, she took another hopping trip to the bathroom, making use of the shower this time. When she emerged fifteen minutes later, she felt better.

Hungry.

She limped over to the bed, threading her fingers through her damp hair, wondering if she should open the connecting door and wave the white flag of truce. There was no reason to be at odds with the man protecting her. Especially considering they would likely be in close proximity for the next five days.

A knock on the door startled her. Not the connecting door, but the main motel-room door. Before she could hobble over to open it, she heard the lock disengage. The door opened, revealing Marc holding a tray of takeout food.

The enticing scent of bacon, eggs and coffee made her mouth water.

"Good morning," he greeted her cautiously, as if trying to gauge her mood. "I thought you might be ready for breakfast."

"I am," she agreed with a tentative smile. "Thanks."

Marc set the tray down on the table and then pulled a white drug-store bag out from beneath his arm. "I bought a bottle of prenatal vitamins as well as some ibuprofen for your ankle."

"I'll take the vitamins," she said, making her way over to the table. "But nothing else."

He opened his mouth as if to argue, but then must have decided against it. "Okay. What about coffee?"

"Decaf," she said with a sigh. She really, really missed regular coffee.

Marc nodded, then crossed over to the small coffee pot located on the dresser to prepare a cup of decaf. Her stomach was rumbling, but she waited for him to return to the table before bowing her head in prayer.

She thanked God for keeping her safe and for the food they were about to eat. She was still new at this prayer stuff, and tried not to fidget beneath Marc's intense gaze.

He waited until she'd opened her disposable container before digging in to his. She unwrapped her plastic silverware and then dug in to her scrambled eggs.

"Delicious," she murmured between bites.

A tiny corner of his mouth lifted in what she suspected was his version of a smile. "I'm glad you like it. I wasn't sure what you preferred, so I got a little of everything."

"I love all breakfast foods," she confessed, nibbling on a slice of toast. "Especially now that I'm not having very much morning sickness."

Instantly, any hint of a smile vanished. "Listen, I think we need to talk about your ex-boyfriend, Vince Ackerman."

Her eggs suddenly tasted like papier-mâché. "Why?"

"I don't remember seeing his name in Detective Barclay's report."

She grimaced and sighed. "So what? I don't see what Vince has to do with anything."

"Didn't any of the officers who questioned you ask about him? Do any sort of investigation into his background?"

"Not that I know of." She was beginning to get annoyed. "They only asked about the robbery details. Then I was only questioned by Detective Barclay and you. No other detectives questioned me. And you were the one who told me that there were almost a dozen bank robberies in a very short time frame. And they all took place after Vince left me. What kind of connection could there be?"

"I'm not sure, but I think we should try to find out."

She wondered what it was like to go through life being suspicious of every little thing. Not the way she wanted to live, that's for sure.

"You can do whatever you like. Personally, I wish that idiot hadn't chosen my window to demand the money. And that the customer hadn't jumped him, jerking his hoodie aside and revealing the tattoo."

"I'm not trying to be difficult," Marc said, obviously sensing her irritation. "It's my job to anticipate the worst-case scenario, every single time."

"I get that. But I don't think Vince is involved."

"What did he do for work?" He finished his eggs and bacon, then started in on the hash browns.

"He was a salesman."

Marc frowned. "What did he sell?"

"Party supplies, trinkets. You know, the kind of thing you might see in corner drugstores."

She lifted a brow. "Not exactly the bank-robber type."

"Probably not. But we also don't know who Terrance Jamison's accomplices were. I can't ignore the remote possibility that Vince was one of them."

"I guess, but I can't see him doing something like that." Although simply talking about what Vince was capable of ruined her appetite. She dropped her half-eaten piece of toast back into the container. "What exactly are you suggesting? That Vince used me to case the bank? That he actually went out to every city where his buddies targeted a bank for the sole purpose of getting one of the tellers to fall in love with him? To propose marriage? That doesn't even make sense." She huffed out a breath. "I'm telling you, the timing is off. He left me days before the first bank was robbed. And from there it was almost another two weeks before my bank was robbed."

"True." Marc took a thoughtful sip of his coffee. "How long were the two of you together?"

"Four months," she murmured. "Don't even say it. I know that's not enough time to get to know a person, but we met at a corner café and he seemed nice, normal, courteous…" Her voice trailed off. Saying the words out loud made her feel like a fool. "I honestly never thought he'd up and disappear along with all the money in our joint account."

"How old is he?"

She grimaced. "Twenty-eight, two years older than me."

"Where did he grow up?"

What was with the twenty questions? "Here in the area—why does it matter? He's gone. His phone has been disconnected, so I don't have a way of contacting him, even if I wanted to."

Marc eyed her over the rim of his cup. "Would it surprise you to know there isn't a Vince Ackerman aged twenty-eight who grew up in the Milwaukee area?"

She stared at him in shock. "How do you know?"

"I did a background check. The only Vince Ackerman in the area is forty-one years old."

That didn't seem possible. Vince might have lied about his age, but no way was he forty-one.

If he hadn't lied about his age, then he must have lied about his name. Or his background. Nausea swirled in her stomach. Just when she'd thought things couldn't get any worse. No doubt the man she'd naively trusted had lied about everything. Including his feelings toward her.

"I'm sorry," Marc said, reaching out to cover her hand with his. "I'm sure this isn't easy to hear."

Yeah and wasn't that the biggest understatement of the year? The gentleness of his hand was reassuring and when he let her go, she missed his warmth. "No, it's not. But none of this means Vince was involved in the bank robbery. Why take all the money out of our joint account if that was part of his plan?"

"Why not? Easy money," Marc said with a shrug.

She swallowed hard, rubbing a hand over her belly in an effort to soothe herself as much as her baby. Stress wasn't good for either of them. Whether Vince was involved in the bank robbery or not didn't matter. She'd already decided to move on with her life.

Once Terrance Jamison was convicted of robbing her at gunpoint and killing the bystander, he'd probably give up the rest of his cohorts in crime in order to get a lighter sentence.

At least, that was the plan.

So why did she feel as if the threads holding everything together were beginning to unravel?

And that Agent Callahan was the only one with the ability to keep it together?

Marc watched the myriad of expressions cross Kari's face, trying to squash a flash of empathy.

He knew, only too well, what if felt like to be betrayed by someone you loved.

Rising to his feet, he stacked their empty

breakfast containers and tossed them in the garbage. When he heard the phone ringing from inside his room, he quickly unlocked the connecting door and rushed over to answer it.

"Hello?"

"It's me," Miles said. "I'm sitting outside the lobby of the motel. What room number are you in?"

"Eight—it's connected to number seven. You have the phones?"

"And extra cash," Miles replied. "I'll be there in two minutes."

It was actually less than that when he heard a sharp rap on his door. Marc opened the door and stepped back, allowing Miles to come in and giving him a brotherly slap on the back.

Miles handed him the bag containing the phones. Marc opened them up and began the tedious process of activating and charging them. They were decent smartphones, with the usual bells and whistles, for which he was grateful.

"Where's your witness?" Miles asked, gesturing toward the open doorway between their rooms. "Is she pretty?"

Marc stifled a sigh. "We're not in high school anymore," he answered drily. "She's a witness, not a potential date."

Miles flashed a knowing grin. "Hey, no reason she can't be both, right?"

Marc shook his head, annoyed by his brother's antics. Girls had generally flocked to Miles instead of him, probably because Marc had always been über-responsible, even back then.

"I'm surprised she didn't come over to meet me," Miles continued.

"She twisted her ankle pretty bad," Marc said. He finished activating the phones then plugged them in, scowling when Miles crossed over to Kari's room.

"Hi, I'm Miles Callahan," he heard his brother say. "It's nice to meet you."

"Kari Danville," she answered in a bemused tone. "Nice to meet you, too."

Marc had to bite the inside of his cheek to keep from lashing out at his brother. So what if Miles was flirting with Kari? It wasn't as if Marc was interested in a personal relationship.

Considering her pregnancy and past history with her ex-fiancé, he doubted she was, either.

"Marc didn't tell me how pretty you are," Miles said with a wink.

"Then we're even, since Marc neglected to tell me how much of a flirt you are."

"I'm not," Miles protested, putting his hand on his chest in protest.

Yeah, he was. Marc hid a smile as he joined them. "Miles was just leaving, weren't you?"

His brother cocked an eyebrow in his direction. "Uh, yeah, sure." Miles grinned. "Do you want me to tell Mom you'll be there for brunch on Sunday? Or do you think the trial will keep you away?"

Marc narrowed his gaze, giving Miles a warning glare. Since their father's murder six months ago, they always tried to get together for church service followed by Sunday brunch. Maybe he hadn't felt God's presence at church, but he always attended anyway. Their mother and Nan expected it. "Not sure, but either way, I'll let Mom know my plans. Thanks again for your help."

"Suit yourself." Miles threw one last smile over his shoulder at Kari. "Nice to meet you, Kari. Hope I see you again sometime soon."

Kari didn't look too impressed. "I doubt it but it's been nice to meet you, too."

"Ouch," Miles muttered, joining Marc in his room. "Shot down in a ball of flames."

Marc wasn't about to waste an ounce of pity for his brother. "Your ego will survive. Take down my new number, in case I need some more help."

Miles jotted down the information, then slipped the scrap of paper into his pocket. "You know, it's been two years since Jess died. It's okay to start dating again."

"What makes you think I haven't?" Marc

countered, having no intention to discuss his personal life, or lack thereof, with anyone. Even his closest brother. "I'll be in touch, okay?"

"Sure thing." Miles opened the door and stepped outside, tossing one more parting shot over his shoulder. "Kari's pretty. I like her."

I like her, too. But of course, he didn't say anything of the sort. Instead he closed the door behind his brother and dragged a hand through his hair.

He knew better than to let Miles get to him. At some point in the last few months, each of his siblings had attempted to play matchmaker.

Efforts that had always backfired.

He was too busy with work to have anything leftover for a relationship, anyway. Hadn't that been the main reason Jessica had cheated on him? Because he was too intense, too serious, too responsible.

The antithesis of fun.

He glanced at his watch, realizing it was almost time to either check out or pay for another night. Considering Kari's ankle, he thought it was probably better to stay put. They hadn't been followed here, and it wouldn't hurt to give her a chance to rest.

The sound of a muffled thud came from her room and he wasted no time in barging over there to see what was going on.

Kari stood on one foot, her injured foot tucked up as if she were a dark-haired stork, staring morosely at the bucket he'd filled with ice a few hours ago. It was lying upside down on the carpet. He ignored the water and bits of ice to reach for her. "Are you all right?"

"You mean other than being a klutz? Yeah, I'm fine," she said, leaning against him.

"Here, let's get you back on the bed to elevate your ankle." He had to fight the urge to lift her into his arms again, making do with anchoring his arm around her waist and helping her close the gap to reach the bed. He found it hard to believe Kari was pregnant, but maybe it was too early for her to show.

He hadn't suspected Jess was three months along, either.

"I was trying to get more ice for my ankle," she said, stretching out on the bedspread.

"I'll get it," he assured her. "Are you sure you can't take some ibuprofen?"

"I'm sure." She tilted her chin stubbornly. "I don't want to take anything that might harm the baby. Besides, it doesn't hurt that much."

He shook his head, knowing that couldn't be true. The skin around her ankle was not only swollen but beginning to turn back and blue as bruising set in. He'd picked up an elastic bandage from the drugstore, along with her vitamins, but he didn't want to use it yet. Better to keep icing it, for now.

"You and your brother seem close," she said as he pressed a towel over the wet spot in the carpet.

He glanced up in surprise. "Yeah, I guess. Miles is just a year younger than me, and there's two and a half years between him and Mitch."

"How many brothers do you have?" she asked, her brown gaze curious.

"Four brothers and a baby sister," he answered, wondering why he was sharing his personal life with her. Maybe because he knew from reading her file that she was all alone in the world. As much as he'd kept to himself over the two years since Jessica's death, he'd always known his family was a phone call away and would drop anything to help him.

The way Miles just had.

"Six in total," Kari echoed in awe. "It must be nice to have so many people in your family."

"Yeah, they're not nosy, bossy, meddling or annoying at all," he said drily.

"Sounds wonderful to me," she said in a soft, wistful voice.

"They are, most of the time," he agreed, silently acknowledging that he wouldn't give up his family for anything. They were the reason he'd taken a position here at the Milwaukee branch of the FBI, when there were other, more prestigious places to work.

He finished cleaning up the mess, then tossed the towels on the bathroom floor before picking up the empty ice bucket. "I was thinking we should stay here another day," he said. "Give your ankle some time to rest."

"No complaints from me." Kari smiled and he knew his brother was wrong. She wasn't just pretty.

She was beautiful, especially when she smiled.

"We're safe here, right?" she added, her brow puckered in a tiny frown.

He pulled himself together. "Yeah, we should be. I'll get some ice, then go to the lobby to pay for another day."

"Sounds good."

He left the motel room and approached the cubicle housing the ice and vending machines. Spending another day here was good for Kari, but not necessarily for investigating the source of the safe house break-in. Although he was fairly sure he'd hear from his boss any minute.

A confrontation he'd rather avoid.

He swept his gaze over the small motel parking lot, taking note of anything out of place. There wasn't so much as a new car parked in the lot, and the traffic on Highway WW seemed light for a Thursday morning.

Satisfied, he carried the ice bucket back inside. After filling a clean towel with ice chips, he draped it over her ankle.

"Be back in a few minutes," he said, turning to retrace his steps. When he opened the door, he paused as a dark SUV complete with tinted windows came flying down the freeway exit ramp, going through a red light. Then he caught a glimpse of the barrel of a gun through the open passenger-side window.

No! They needed to move.

Now.

He barged back inside the hotel. "Kari, grab your stuff. We need to get out of here."

To her credit she didn't argue. She sat up, tossed the ice pack aside and then grabbed her vitamins. Instead of putting her shoes on, she carried them, wincing as she limped toward him.

He grabbed the laptop computer and his keys. They exited the motel and jumped into the car.

Marc hit the gas and sped out of the parking lot.

Despite his sixty-second head start, he could see the SUV was hot on his tail.

How had they found him? Not through Miles.

His boss? He didn't want to believe it.

"They're gaining on us," Kari whispered, as she struggled to get her left foot into her shoe.

Crack!

The sound of gunfire had him planting his foot to the floor, pushing the car engine as fast as it would go.

Another gunshot echoed and he gripped the steering wheel tighter.

He couldn't bear the thought of failing Kari and her baby. He had to figure out a way to keep them safe from harm.

Because there was no way he could cope with another death on his conscience.

FOUR

Clutching the door handle with a white-knuckled grip, Kari tried to keep her head down as she stared in horrified shock at the side mirror and the large black SUV keeping pace behind them.

Dear Lord, keep us safe!

"Call for help," Marc said in a terse voice.

Tearing her gaze from the mirror, she searched for the new disposable phones his brother had purchased earlier that morning. She grabbed the device and pushed the 9-1-1 digits with trembling fingers.

The phone rang several times before the dispatcher picked up. "What's your emergency?"

"We're heading north of the interstate on Highway WW and there's a black SUV with tinted windows shooting at us."

"Is anyone injured?"

"Not yet!" Kari sucked in a harsh breath when another crack echoed through the air. Their car skidded for a moment on a slippery spot on the asphalt before Marc wrestled it back on the road. "Hurry!"

"I'm sending squads to your area. Please stay on the line."

"I'll try." She swallowed hard when Marc pulled out his weapon.

"Grab the wheel," he ordered.

Making a decision between the phone and the car wasn't that difficult. Kari dropped the device in the center console and grabbed onto the steering wheel with both hands, doing her best to keep it steady. Her heart thundered in her chest as she stared at the recently plowed blacktop highway.

Marc rolled down the window and poked out his head and his gun to return fire.

The gunshot blasts were excruciatingly loud, seeming to reverberate through the vehicle. She winced and struggled to keep the car centered on the road.

Marc ducked back inside and took control of the driving once again. She heard the voice of the 911 operator asking questions so she picked up the phone again.

"Sorry...can you repeat that?" Kari asked.

"I need the name of the closest exit," the dispatcher said. "I have two Washington County Sheriff's deputies dispatched to your location but I need to provide more details."

"We're driving a dark blue four-door Camry," she told the woman. She peered through the windshield, trying to find a distinguishing landmark amidst the snow-covered farmer's fields. "There! We just passed Silver Lake Road."

"That helps, hang on."

Kari glanced over at Marc, who was dividing his attention between the road and his rearview mirror. Thankfully, there weren't too many cars on the road. She stifled a scream as he leaned on the horn, barreling through yet another intersection without hesitation.

"The police will be here soon," she told him.

"They'd better hurry," he muttered in a grim tone.

Another gunshot rang out and this time there was an answering thud. Their car swerved sharply as the bullet found its mark.

"We're hit," she told the dispatcher. "You have to hurry!"

"My foot is all the way down to the floor," Marc said, and she didn't bother to tell him she'd meant for the dispatcher to work faster.

The landscape zipping past the window was making her dizzy, but it still wasn't fast enough to put more distance between their car and the darkly tinted SUV. Kari didn't want to think about what would happen if they didn't find a way to escape the gunmen on their tail.

"Wait a minute, do you hear that?" Marc asked abruptly.

At first she didn't know what he was talking about, but then she heard it, too. Sirens. Police sirens.

Help was on the way!

The SUV suddenly slowed down and made a dangerously sharp left-hand turn. She closed her eyes, silently thanking God for watching over them.

"Tell the dispatcher the SUV is headed west," Marc urged. "They have to find it."

She repeated what he'd told her to the dispatcher, but the woman cut her off. "So you're not in danger anymore?"

Kari was still in danger, and would be until she testified, but didn't think that was terribly relevant. "That's correct…the SUV is no longer behind us."

Marc had taken his foot off the accelerator, too, and the car dropped down to a reasonable speed. He turned right, heading east in the opposite direction the SUV had taken, then he reached over to take the phone from her hand, pushing the button to disconnect from the call.

She gasped. "Why did you do that?"

"I'm sorry, but we can't waste time talking to the deputies right now."

"But don't you want to find the SUV that was shooting at us?"

"Yeah, I do. Especially since we don't know how they found us in the first place." He scowled and executed another turn. "First the safe house and now this? Not a coincidence. There has to be some sort of inside leak and that means being interviewed by the sheriff's deputies is not an option. Not until I know who we can trust."

Her mouth went dry at the thought of someone in law enforcement being entangled in this mess. "Do you really think that's possible?"

He shrugged. "I can't eliminate the possibility. My top priority is keeping you safe."

Difficult to argue with his logic, since she wanted the exact same thing. She placed a soothing hand over her rounded stomach and let out a heavy sigh. "I don't want you to get in trouble."

The corner of his mouth tipped up in a crooked grin. "Don't worry about me, Kari. Right now we need to find a place to hide. Keep your eyes peeled for even the most remote possibilities."

She stared out the passenger-side window, not sure what he meant. The snow-covered farmers' fields didn't offer many hiding spots. The houses were few and far between.

They should have stayed in the city.

"There," Marc said, his tone rich with satisfaction. "That will work for now."

She frowned, looking around in confusion. There wasn't anything around other than a large seemingly abandoned and rather dilapidated red barn located a few yards in from the road. "Are you sure this is a good idea?"

"I hope so." He slowed the car and turned into the rutted gravel driveway leading to the structure. The car bounced and jostled as he crept closer. Then he threw the gearshift into Park, but left the engine running.

"I'm going to open the barn doors and you're going to drive inside, okay?"

"All right." She unbuckled her seat belt and then awkwardly climbed over the center console to get into the driver's seat. She fumbled for the button to adjust the seat, moving it forward until her right foot reached the pedal.

Marc worked quickly, opening the doors just wide enough for her to drive inside. The minute she cleared the threshold, he began closing the doors behind her. She watched in the rearview mirror, frowning when she noticed he didn't close them all the way. He disappeared for several long moments before returning inside. This time, he closed the doors tightly.

Darkness surrounded them, forcing her to turn on the headlights.

Marc opened the passenger-side door and rummaged in the glove box, taking out a flashlight and testing the batteries. "I'm going to see if I can find some sort of tracking device on the vehicle. Sit tight for a few minutes."

She huddled behind the wheel as Marc examined the car. The task seemed to take forever before he returned. "Okay, turn off the engine."

She switched off the headlights and twisted the key, shutting down the car. Then she scooted back over to the passenger-side seat, giving him room to get inside.

"Did you find anything?"

"No."

"Now what?" she asked, trying to read his facial expression in the darkness.

"We wait."

She shivered, even though the temperature inside the vehicle was relatively warm. At least for the moment. "For how long?"

He skimmed his hand over his short brown hair and let out a sigh. "For as long as it takes."

Kari didn't like that answer, but what could she say? Arguing wasn't going to help. And hiding from gunmen wasn't exactly her forte. She had to have faith, to trust that Marc knew what he was doing.

She shivered again, and he reached out to put his hand on her arm. "You okay?"

"Yes." Even through her winter jacket, his

touch had the ability to calm her nerves. Not just because he was armed.

But because she liked him. Trusted him. Not only with her life, but with that of her unborn child.

She felt safe in his care.

Marc wished he knew how on earth they'd been found at the motel. Miles would never put him in harm's way, and being a detective, his brother was smart enough to make sure he wasn't followed to the motel. He hadn't found a tracking device, either, so the only logical possibility was that somehow their location had been traced through the voice-mail message that Marc had left for his boss.

Obviously, returning to the Ravenswood Motel wasn't an option, but he also didn't like the fact that the SUV had followed his car. He had no way of knowing if they'd managed to trace his license-plate number.

He'd feel better if they were able to obtain a new car as soon as possible.

For now, however, they were well hidden inside the ramshackle barn.

Even surrounded by darkness and the musty scent of stale hay, Marc was hyperaware of Kari sitting beside him. Her cranberry-vanilla scent reminded him of the upcoming Christmas holiday.

Normally, he volunteered to work over the holiday. He didn't have a wife or children like so many of the other agents did and keeping busy helped pass the time. Granted, he usually spent Christmas with his mom, Nan and siblings, but that wasn't the same as having a family of his own.

Oddly enough, the holiday season was about the only time he missed Jessica. At least the early years of their marriage, when they'd cuddled by the fire, sipping hot apple cider and talking about their future.

But then things changed. Not all at once, but little by little over time. At first Jess complained about the hours he spent working, then their arguments became more frequent, especially surrounding his disinterest in attending parties that lasted way into the night.

His mistake was encouraging her to go out without him.

A mistake that had ultimately cost Jess her life, along with the baby she carried. Identifying his wife in the morgue had been the hardest thing he'd ever done.

Slamming a door against the gut-wrenching memories, Marc forced himself to focus on the present. He needed to figure out how he was going to keep Kari safe while continuing his investigation. He felt Kari shivering beside him, so he reached up intending to start the engine.

Kari stopped him by covering his hand with hers. "Don't," she said in a low voice. "I don't think running the car in an enclosed space is a good idea."

The softness of her hand was momentarily distracting. His emotions had been in a deep freeze for years, so why were they thawing for Kari now? He gave himself a mental shake and pointed through the windshield. "See the open spaces up in the loft? They're enough to prevent the exhaust fumes from building up to a dangerous level."

"I'd rather not take any chances with the baby," she protested.

He didn't necessarily agree, but dropped his hand from the key and turned toward her. "All right, then scoot closer and lean against me as much as you can. Staying close together will maintain our body heat."

The console between the seats prevented them from getting too close, but he managed to get his muscular arm around her slim shoulders, sharing a bit of body warmth. She held herself tensely at first, but then relaxed enough to rest her head against his shoulder.

"How long do we have to stay here?" she asked.

"As long as we can stand it." The coldness

of winter would push them to move before he liked, considering the longer they could remain hidden, the better off they would be. The Washington County Sheriff's deputies would be on the lookout for them over the next twenty-four hours, along with the SUV that had been shooting at them, but Marc hoped to slip out of the county before that happened.

Of course, the deputies here would likely put all the surrounding counties on notice, as well. And even though they were victims, he knew the police would still want to question them.

"Marc? Is there any way for me to avoid testifying in court?"

He frowned at her question. "Listen, Kari, I'm going to keep you safe, okay?"

She didn't say anything for a long moment. "I know you're going to do your best, but I just wondered if my testimony was really all that critical to the case."

He understood why she wanted out of this mess, but refusing to testify? He swallowed a surge of unease. "Yes, we do need your testimony. Jamison's tattoo was a major factor in his arrest. You're our key witness. Not only did you see the tattoo, but you drew it so that the officers could recognize it. I know you're scared, especially after everything you've been through, but we need you to do this, Kari. We need you to testify against Jamison."

She let out a heavy sigh. "I know. I just thought…" her voice trailed off.

He wished he could see her expression clearly. "Taking you off the witness list doesn't guarantee that you'd be safe. I believe Jamison's accomplices would still come after you in an attempt to silence you once and for all." He hated making her more afraid, but she needed to understand the full extent of the danger she faced.

"Okay, I get it. I'm in danger either way." Her voice held a note of defeat and he wished he could think of some way to cheer her up.

"I made a mistake at the motel. I called and left a voice-mail message for my boss, Special Agent in Charge Evan White. I don't think Evan betrayed me, but he might have mentioned my location to someone else within the bank-robbery task force."

"I can't believe someone within the group is involved in this," Kari murmured.

"I don't like it, either," he admitted gruffly. "But regardless, we're on our own now. I'm severing all ties to the task force. The only other thing we need to do is ditch this car—then we'll be safe."

"I like the sound of that," she agreed.

A companionable silence fell between them. Marc couldn't help being impressed by Kari's resilience after the close call with the black SUV. There weren't too many women who could take something like that in stride.

Kari's breathing deepened and he realized she'd fallen asleep. The only two things he knew about pregnancy was the tendency toward morning sickness and fatigue. He was glad she was able to rest, but after a couple of hours, she began to shiver in the cold.

"I think it's probably safe to get back on the road," Marc said. He twisted the key in the ignition, ignoring her immediate protest. "I'm heading out to open the barn doors now. Can you crawl back in to the driver's seat?"

"Y-yes."

Marc climbed back out of the car and strode toward the heavy barn doors. He pried them open about a foot, peering out to make sure there were no cops around. Dark clouds swirled overhead, bringing the threat of snow.

There were a couple cars on the highway, but nothing too alarming, so he widened the opening enough so that Kari could drive through.

When she'd pulled clear of the doorway, he closed the barn and returned to the car.

Marc continued to make his way southeast,

searching for a safe place to stay. As the car ate up the miles without any sign of the police, he began to relax. Kari's stomach rumbled loudly and he realized the hour was well past lunch-time.

"We'll get something to eat soon," he said. "But I want to find another motel first."

"I understand." She held her hand over her stomach, an unconscious protective gesture he noticed she used often.

Less than an hour later, he saw a sign advertising a lodge called the Cottage Grove Motel. There was a fast-food restaurant located nearby, so he pulled in and they ordered lunch to go.

When they reached the motel, he checked in and asked for connecting rooms. The clerk was able to accommodate his request, and soon they were seated inside at a small table ready to eat their lunch.

Marc hesitated when Kari bowed her head to pray, then followed suit. He found himself silently thanking God for protecting them, feeling a connection to his faith for the first time since Jessica had died.

Eating the simple meal didn't take long and when he finished cleaning up the remnants, he found Kari doodling on the motel stationary.

He watched her for several moments while her drawing took shape.

"Wait a minute, is that me?" he asked in surprise.

She grimaced. "Yes, although I'm not very good at portraits."

"I disagree. You're very good—the level of detail is amazing." She'd captured everything—his eyes, his facial structure, even the faint scar above his right eyebrow, a gift from Miles, who'd pushed him onto a coffee table when they were young.

"Thanks, but there are a lot of people who are much more talented than I am."

He wasn't so sure about that, but then was struck by an idea. "Wait a minute, can you draw Vince for me?"

She dropped the pencil and pushed the paper aside. "Why would I want to do that? I told you, he's not involved in this."

"You're right, it's not likely he's involved, but he still stole money from you. I'd like to at least figure out his real name."

Kari sat for a moment, then abruptly pushed up from the small table with an agitated motion, standing lopsided as she avoided putting weight on her injured ankle. She picked up the paper and pencil. "I'd rather forget about him.

Excuse me." She limped through the connecting door to her room, leaving him staring after her in confusion.

Why didn't she want justice? Why not hold Vince Ackerman, or whatever his name was, accountable for his actions?

Then again, maybe just the thought of seeing him again was too upsetting for her.

Unpacking his computer, Marc tried to focus instead on the immediate threat of the gunmen in the SUV. He needed a new vehicle and to figure out where the leak was coming from, before there was another attempt on Kari's life.

But deep down, he couldn't stop thinking about how much he wanted to find the man who'd hurt Kari and bring him to justice.

FIVE

Kari sat on the edge of the bed, staring at the sketch she'd done of Marc Callahan.

He didn't seem to understand that she didn't want to find Vince. Didn't want him to know about the baby for fear that he'd try to get visitation rights. The last thing she needed was a constant reminder of how foolish and naive she'd been.

It just didn't seem possible that her ex was involved in the bank robberies. Although, if he was, being arrested and tossed in jail would be to her advantage.

She swung around to sit propped up against the headboard, elevating her injured ankle. It was still painfully swollen and looked terrible. She hoped she hadn't torn any ligaments or anything else serious enough to need surgery.

Picking up her notepad, she began sketching the tattoo she'd glimpsed on Jamison's chest. It was easier to draw than to describe in words—

a cobra curled around a samurai sword dripping with blood, along with a grotesque mask of a warrior with slanted but vacant eyes.

She wondered what the tattoo meant to Jamison. A badge of courage? A medal of honor? Or something else, like being part of a gang, or a group of warriors? Had Marc and his task force found anyone else with a similar inked drawing?

If so, he hadn't shared that information with her. Not too surprising, considering she was a witness and not privy to inside information related to the ongoing bank-robbery investigation.

Kari closed her eyes, her mind flashing back to the day Jamison had approached her window. It was late September and hot outside, yet he'd been wearing a sweatshirt, the hood pulled up over his head, and she remembered feeling a shiver of apprehension at the time, sensing something wasn't right. Since so many people used electronic banking, the place wasn't very busy, especially at closing time on a Monday. Her window had been the only one open, and the young man in his early twenties had just left her station when Jamison approached.

At the time, it seemed everything happened so fast. The robber had told her he had a gun and to hand over all the high-denomination cash in the drawer. She remembered pushing the panic button that gave off a silent alarm, before pulling out the money he'd demanded.

The young man must have heard something, because suddenly he shouted and grabbed Jamison's arm, pulling the hoodie over to the side with enough force that the zipper came down, revealing the tank top he wore underneath. The tattoo was high on his shoulder, in plain sight.

Jamison shot the kid, grabbed the money and bolted out the door, disappearing from the bank before the police could arrive.

She'd given him all hundred-dollar bills, so he'd gotten away with a fair amount of cash. Still, it was a far cry from the hundreds and thousands of dollars you often heard about in these types of robberies.

The samurai sword and cobra tattoo was their only clue other than Jamison himself. She'd heard that Jamison wasn't talking to the authorities, and again, she thought about the tattoo. If he was in some sort of samurai-warrior gang, it could be that he'd rather do jail time than rat out his accomplices.

Kari opened her eyes, trying to rein in her whirling thoughts. The young man who'd grabbed Jamison had died from the gunshot wound to his chest. She prayed for his family, whoever they were, every night. He shouldn't have grabbed Jamison, shouldn't have died in a misguided attempt to help. But there was no denying that Jamison would have likely eluded the police if she hadn't glimpsed his tattoo.

Thinking about the young man who'd died that day made her pick up the paper and pencil she'd taken from Marc's room. With sure strokes, she sketched Vince's face. If there was any possibility, no matter how remote, that he was involved, she wanted Marc's task force to find him.

And if Vince wasn't involved, she'd hope and pray he had no interest in her or their baby.

When she finished the sketch, she slid out of bed and hobbled over to the doorway between their rooms. She noticed he was talking on the phone.

"Mitch, it's Marc. I need to borrow your buddy's car. Call me at the following number as soon as possible." He rattled off the number for his new phone then disconnected from the call and glanced over at her.

"Here…this is what Vince looks like." She held out the drawing and Marc quickly crossed over to take it. "Mitch is another one of your brothers, right?"

"Yeah, I'm sure he's at work, but hopefully he'll call me soon." He raked his gaze over her sketch. "This is great, thanks. I'll send this to

Miles, see if he can dig up something on this guy's real identity."

She shrugged, holding on to the door frame for support. "What about Jamison's tattoo? Was your task force able to find out anything about it?"

"Sit down. You need to stay off that ankle." He gestured toward the small round table she'd abandoned earlier, so she hopped over. "We ran the tattoo through the FBI criminal-investigation database but didn't come up with anything specific. Why?"

"Images from that day keep rolling through my mind. It seems like the design might mean something."

"Try not to worry about it," he suggested. "I'm here to keep you safe."

A flash of irritation made her grit her teeth. "It's obvious Jamison's accomplices want to silence me once and for all. Don't you think it's better if we figure out who they are before that happens?"

He leaned forward, capturing her hands in his. "Kari, the task force has been working the case for weeks since Jamison's arrest, even before that, from the time the first bank was robbed. So far, we having nothing that indicates the tattoo symbolizes a gang."

"What else do you know about Jamison?" she

asked, drawing strength from the warmth of his hands. "I wonder if the Samurai tattoo indicates he has a Japanese heritage."

"Yeah, we have considered that, but the information doesn't help us much. We checked into the Japanese gangs in Chicago but they don't use the samurai symbol—they use dragons."

"I guess that makes sense."

"I think we're better off focusing on the leak within the task force," Marc added, releasing her hands.

"Is it possible one of them has a tattoo?"

He shrugged. "Not that we're aware of. To be fair, it's not that difficult to hide one."

"Figures," she lamented with a sigh. Her gaze fell on a slip of paper where Marc had written out five names, and she quickly figured out they were the other members of the task force.

Detective Steve Young, Detective Jason Wu, Detective Monique Barclay, Agent Angela Wright and Agent David Hermes.

Was Wu a Japanese name? Or Chinese? Did it matter? Anyone could get a Samurai tattoo.

Marc rose to his feet. "I'm going to fax a copy of your drawing of Vince to Miles. I'll be back shortly."

"Sure." Kari swallowed the urge to snatch the sketch and tear it into little pieces as he left the motel room. A cold blast of air made her shiver.

Being alone in the motel room made her feel on edge. They'd been on the run for what seemed like forever instead of just over twenty-four hours.

Today was Thursday. There had already been two attempts on her life in the past twenty-four hours. In less than five days, she'd have to testify in federal court against Terrance Jamison.

Days that would seem like a lifetime.

She closed her eyes and prayed. *Lord, please guide us to safety.*

Marc used the tiny motel business center to send the fax to Miles's home office, then made his way back to his motel room. Light snow-flakes drifted in the air, melting into tiny drops of water the moment they hit his skin.

He'd parked the car behind the building, so that it wasn't visible from the road. He'd also backed it in, so that they could get away quickly if needed.

There was a nagging itch along the back of his neck, warning him that they wouldn't be safe until he got rid of his car. Anyone from within the task force could easily find out what he was driving. The snowy weather was hardly a deterrent.

For a moment his gut tightened at the thought of his family being in danger. He didn't like it any more than he liked the fact that Kari was the ultimate target here. He'd prefer he be the one they were after because he knew he could take care of himself.

Of course, most of his family worked within some sort of law enforcement, except for Mike, and he was a private investigator with a license to carry a weapon. To make a move against any of them would be foolish.

No, he had to believe his family was safe. His brothers and his sister at the DA's office wouldn't give up without seeking justice.

Although he was forced to admit that despite their efforts, his father's murderer was still out there somewhere.

Marc paused at the door, turning back to sweep his gaze over the motel parking lot, making sure the same vehicles from when they arrived were still there. They were, and no new ones had joined them, either.

Opening the door, he stomped the snow off his feet and let himself in. Kari was still sitting at the small table, but she'd opened his computer and was doing some sort of search on the internet.

He crossed over to see what she was doing. She glanced up at him. "I tried a search on samurai gangs, but came up empty."

The corner of his mouth kicked up in a smile.

"Yeah, we can't assume there is any connection between the tattoo and the Japanese people."

She grimaced. "You're right. I just thought…" Her voice trailed off.

"I know you're trying to help, but maybe you should leave the investigating to me."

"There's no reason I can't lend a hand."

Marc wasn't sure what to say to that, since there really wasn't anything she could do to help, but his new phone rang, so he quickly answered it. "Callahan."

"It's Miles. Where are you?"

Marc's body tensed at the tone of his brother's voice. "At a new location, why? What's going on?"

"I picked up a tail."

Marc clenched his free hand into a fist. "When? After you left us at the Ravenswood Motel?"

"No, I went from the motel to work, but noticed the tail when I left. Took me a while to get rid of it, too."

Marc swallowed hard. "They found us at Ravenswood. We just barely managed to get away."

His brother muttered something incomprehensible under his breath. "I don't like it," Miles said. "I didn't see any indication I was being followed on my way to drop off the phones. There wasn't a lot of traffic… I'm sure I would have spotted a tail."

"I'm not blaming you," Marc assured him. "Besides, it doesn't matter—we're safe for now. I've left a message for Mitch. I want a different set of wheels and you know he's housing his buddy's truck in his garage while the guy is overseas."

"Yeah, borrowing Garrett's truck is a great idea. Did Mitch call you back?"

"Not yet."

"I'll see if I can reach him. Could be that he ignored your call because of the strange number," Miles said. "I agree with you—the sooner you get a different vehicle, the better."

"Thanks. And Miles? I faxed a drawing to your home office. The guy was going by the name Vince Ackerman, his age roughly in his late twenties or early thirties. I couldn't find anyone by that name in the area, so it could be that he's using an alias."

"You think he's involved?"

Marc hesitated. "Not sure, but I'd still be interested in finding him even if he's not."

"I'll see what I can do."

"Thanks. Be careful, Miles. I don't like the fact that you're being watched."

"Don't worry, I can take care of myself. I'll alert the rest of the family, too, just in case. I'll be in touch."

Marc disconnected from the call, not liking

the turn of events one bit. Once Mitch brought him a different car, he'd make sure to stay far away from his family. No sense in dragging them into his mess.

"Is Miles okay?" Kari asked softly.

"He's fine." Logically, Marc knew that his brother was a good cop, a savvy detective. Still, it made him uneasy knowing that he'd dragged his brother into danger. "As soon as I hear from Mitch, we'll get out of here."

Her eyes widened in surprise. "We're not staying the night? Didn't you pay for the rooms already?"

"No, we're not staying overnight and I don't care about the money. We'll find somewhere else to go once we have alternate transportation."

Kari looked as if she was about to argue, but then nodded. "Okay. Sounds good."

Marc gathered what little they had, mainly their coats, his computer and Kari's drawings, into a small pile on the table. He slid the sketch Kari had drawn of him into his pocket. A bit of sentimental foolishness? Maybe. But he didn't take it back out, either.

Staring at his phone waiting for Mitch to call didn't make the phone ring any faster, so he continued his internet search. Kari sat next to him, and he tried not be distracted by her cranberry-vanilla scent.

Why did she smell like home?

"How well do you know the task-force members?" she asked.

It was a good question. "Not very well at all," he admitted. "I did work with Detective Steve Young in the past, but the other two detectives I barely know at all. I know the other federal agents, but Angela Wright is new to the Milwaukee office, so this is the first case we've worked together. Hermes has been around for the last couple of years. He's a bit of a hot dog, always trying to show off, but I can't imagine him, or any of them really, getting caught up in something like this."

"I didn't think Vince would up and leave me, either, taking all the money out of our account with him, but he did. Sometimes we don't know people as well as we thought."

"Yeah, I know." Marc didn't like it, but he had little choice but to accept the facts as they were. "It's clear that someone with inside information is involved, so that means either my boss, or one of these task-force members is the leak."

"Where do we start?"

He stared at the names on his list, trying to imagine which one was hiding a secret life, a criminal connection. His phone rang, startling him. "Callahan."

"I hear you're in trouble," his brother Mitch said, getting straight to the point.

"Yeah, you could say that. I need to borrow Garrett's truck until Monday afternoon. My witness is testifying first thing Monday morning, as soon as they pick a jury."

"No problem. Where do you want to meet?"

Marc knew he was blessed to have such a supportive family. "I'm about fifteen minutes east of Madison. How about we meet at the outlet stores in thirty minutes?"

"I should be able to manage that," his brother agreed.

"Might want to bring Miles along. I'm not sure using my car is a good idea."

"Okay, see you in a half hour."

Marc was glad to be able to move, to take the next step in assuring Kari's safety. He shut down the computer, then held up her coat so she could slide into it.

"Thanks," she murmured, drawing the edges close to zip it up. He wondered how much longer she'd fit in normal clothes, then reminded himself that her wardrobe was hardly his concern.

He shrugged into his own coat and then tucked the computer under his arm. He left the room keys on the table, then held out his arm so she could lean against him as they made their way through Kari's room toward the door leading outside.

Before opening the door, he peered through the window, glancing at the parking lot. Nothing had changed, except the snow was falling faster now, collecting on the parked cars and covering the asphalt. "Let's go, but stay to my left, okay?"

They left the motel, moving slower than he liked, keeping close to the building as they rounded the corner to the back. His car was also covered in snow, and once Kari was safe inside, he quickly cleared the windows before joining her.

She didn't say much as he drove away from the motel, although he could tell she was watching the road behind them for any sign of the SUV. He hated knowing she was so afraid.

He headed for the interstate, but they were on the freeway for barely ten minutes when bright headlights gained on them from behind. Marc tensed when he realized the vehicle was an SUV.

The same one as before? How was that possible?

He hit the gas, determined to put distance between them. At three o'clock in the afternoon, it was still light out, but visibility wasn't great because of the snow.

"Gun!" Kari shouted. Sure enough, he could

see the narrow barrel of a gun poking through the passenger-side window just like it had earlier.

"Hang on," he said, pushing the speed limit as much as he dared.

"Not again! Please, Lord, not again!"

Kari's desperate cry stabbed like a hot poker in his gut. He'd promised to keep her safe.

He couldn't bear the thought of failure. Of losing another witness.

A pregnant witness.

SIX

Kari couldn't believe they'd been found again so quickly. She mentally braced herself for more gunfire, wondering if this time the bullets would find their mark.

Crack! Crack!

This time, the car didn't swerve, giving her the impression that they hadn't been hit. Marc was doing his best to get away, but the roads were slick with snow and she could tell from the side window that the black SUV was closing the gap behind them.

Suddenly, she was overcome by a wave of fury. The heavy-duty scraper he'd used to clean off the car was lying across the floor at her feet. She grabbed it, then released her seat belt.

"What are you doing?" Marc hissed. "You need to stay buckled in."

She ignored him, kneeling now on the seat and then reaching behind to hit the button to open the sunroof. She shoved the ice scraper up through the opening. Hanging on to the handle she threw it against the wind directly at the SUV on their tail with every bit of strength she possessed. It sailed through the air, then found its mark.

Thwack!

Her mouth dropped open in shock when she saw the windshield of the SUV morph into a spiderweb of cracks, enough that it must have affected the driver's ability to see as the car swerved wildly on the road and then dropped back.

As she slid back down into her seat Marc stomped on the brake, cranked the steering wheel hard to the left, and drove through an opening in the median. Instantly, they were headed in the opposite direction on the interstate, leaving the SUV behind.

"I can't believe you risked your neck like that," he said as he took the first exit to get off the freeway. "But I have to admit, that was incredible."

"I was just so mad," she said, as if that explained everything. "I wanted them to go away and to leave us alone."

His smile faded. "I checked for some sort of tracker, but maybe I missed it. I don't know how else they could have found us so quickly. We were barely fifteen minutes away from the motel."

"At least we weren't stuck there, like last time," she said with a weary sigh. "God must be watching out for us."

"I guess I can't argue with that," Marc agreed, much to her surprise. She'd noticed that he didn't lean on prayer the way she did; granted he'd wait for her to finish praying, but he never participated. Yet it sounded as if his family was close and attended church regularly. She wondered what happened to make Marc turn away from faith. "We can't get rid of this car fast enough."

"It's great that your brothers are willing to help out."

"Yeah, I'm fortunate to have them." He glanced over at her. "They'll protect you, too, Kari. If anything happens to me, I want you to call one of my brothers."

She frowned. "Nothing is going to happen to you. Or to me."

"I know, but humor me. Take my phone and enter their numbers into yours, just in case."

"Fine." She didn't like it, but it gave her something to do while he drove. He was staying off the main highway now, and the less traveled country roads were more treacherous, slowing their progress. "Should we stop and try to find whatever is on the car?"

"I considered doing that, but since I couldn't find it before, not sure I want to try again. Besides, their current ride is out of commission, thanks to you, so I think it's better to just get to the outlet mall. It's not that far."

When she finished entering his brothers' numbers, she set the phone back in the center console. The rush of adrenaline faded, leaving her feeling shaky and queasy.

All this stress couldn't be good for the baby.

She took several slow, deep breaths in an effort to calm her racing heart. Closing her eyes, she tried to imagine the sound of the ocean, waves lapping at the shoreline. Feeling better, she opened her eyes and tried not to get discouraged by the continual onslaught of snow.

"The mall is five miles up ahead," Marc said in an encouraging tone. "We're almost there."

She nodded. "Great."

"Are you all right?" he asked as if sensing her inner turmoil.

"Yes, although I'll be better once we're truly safe."

He frowned, glancing at her midsection, before turning his eyes back to the road. "You're not having any cramping or other problems, are you?"

"Nothing like that," she assured him. "Just trying to relax, that's all."

He nodded and didn't say anything more until they reached the outlet mall. In spite of the snow, there were a shocking number of cars in the parking lot, die-hard shoppers desperate to snag a few good deals before Christmas. Off to one corner she could see a large, dark-colored truck parked right next to a smaller cherry-red Jeep.

Marc drove straight over, no doubt recognizing his brother's car. She found herself hoping they'd get the truck; at least they wouldn't get stuck in the snow.

As they rolled to a stop, the driver's side doors of both vehicles opened and two tall men got out, hunching against the wind. They came right over to Marc's car.

She recognized Miles, smiling as he opened her door and poked his head inside. "You're late. Everything okay?"

"Yeah. Thanks to Kari's quick thinking we managed to get away from our tail."

Miles let out a whistle. "What did she do?"

Marc grinned. "Tossed the ice scraper and shattered their windshield."

"Nice job," Miles said with clear admiration in his tone.

The other man whom she assumed was Mitch had opened Marc's door. "How did they find you?"

"I looked once already, but I'm thinking there must be some sort of tracking device on my car," Marc said, picking up his phone from the center console and tucking it into his pocket. "I'm planning to leave it here because I don't want anyone from the family driving it."

"We'll see if we can find the device. If not, we'll do as you suggested. These are the keys to Garrett's truck," Mitch said, handing a bulky key fob to Marc. "Garrett is pretty attached to it, so try not to wreck anything, okay?"

"I'll do my best," Marc said grimly. "And if anything happens, I'll take care of it."

"Need a hand, Kari?" Miles said, holding out his hand for her. "How's that ankle?"

"Sore," she admitted. She took Miles's hand and allowed him to help her out of the car. Marc's brother was a harmless flirt and she suspected that if he knew she was pregnant, he'd disappear faster than she could blink. It made her smile to imagine his reaction.

"Grab the computer, would you, Mitch?" Marc said brusquely as he came around the front of the car to meet her. He put his arm around her waist. "I'll take it from here, bro."

"Sure thing," Miles replied in a tone edged with humor. He dropped Kari's arm and gave her a sly wink. She rolled her eyes at his antics. "Take good care of your witness, Marc. And let us know if you need anything else."

"Will do." Marc helped her over to the huge

truck. It was so high off the ground she wondered how she'd manage to get in.

Marc opened the passenger-side door, then must have noticed the same issue as he planted his hands around her waist. "Hang on," he advised. She braced her hands on his shoulders as he easily lifted her up and into the seat.

"Thanks," she murmured, hoping her cheeks weren't turning too pink, and if they were, that his brothers would blame the snow.

He smiled at her and nodded, waiting for her to swing her feet inside before shutting the door. As she sat shivering for a moment she was startled to realize just how handsome Marc was when he smiled.

Too bad he didn't do it more often.

Mitch opened the back door and set the computer on the seat. He nodded in her direction but didn't say anything more. It seemed that Mitch had a more serious nature, much like Marc's and a complete opposite of the flirtatious Miles.

And what about the other members of Marc's family? She found herself curious about them, as well, especially his sister.

What had it been like to grow up with five older brothers? She imagined they were protective of their baby sister and wondered if their macho attitude had driven his sister crazy, or if she'd appreciated their willingness to stand up for her.

Kari would have liked having brothers around when she was growing up. But there was no sense in wishing for something she'd never have. Maybe someday she'd find someone who wouldn't mind the fact that she had a baby by another man. And if not, that was okay, too.

At least that's what she told herself. But she knew that even though she could try to be the best possible mother, her child would always miss having a father.

The same way she'd missed having one.

"Thanks for the help," Marc said as he slapped his brothers on the back. "Keep in touch. I don't like thinking that you'll be followed."

"We can handle it," Mitch assured him. "And if you need anything, let us know."

"I will." Marc made his way back to the truck and quickly climbed in. "All set?" he asked Kari as he cranked the key, bringing the rumbling engine to life.

"Of course." She'd already latched her seat belt. In the rearview mirror he watched as his brothers circled his car, checking along the wheel well, searching for the tracker.

As much as he wanted to stay and find the device himself, his priority right now was to get

Kari someplace safe. Which meant getting away from the outlet mall.

"Heated seats!" she exclaimed in surprise, putting her hand over the tiny pores in the leather.

"It's a luxury, isn't it?"

She nodded. "So now what? Where are we going?"

"Another motel, I'm afraid." He wished there was another option.

"At least we'll finally be safe," she murmured, relaxing against the leather cushion.

"Yeah." Marc was relieved that they would no longer be in danger. However, he still needed to figure out who from the task force was after them.

And unfortunately, he didn't have any clue where to start. The thought that someone he worked with could be involved was unfathomable.

But there wasn't any other explanation.

Logically, Marc knew that it could be any one of them, so he needed to find out who might be in trouble—financially, professionally or personally.

Yeah, sure. Easier said than done.

He drove through the snow, watching road signs for a potential place to stay. The decision to head east toward Milwaukee was a practical one. Since no one could find him through Garrett Rolland's truck, he figured it would be best to stay closer to the city, since that was where the task-force members were located.

"How about that place?" Kari asked, breaking into his thoughts. "The Silent Knight Motel? It has Wi-Fi and a restaurant across the street."

"Why not?" They'd been driving for less than an hour, but maybe she was hungry again.

The Wi-Fi would come in handy, even though he'd rather use a secure server. Taking the next exit, he found the motel without difficulty and once again went in to obtain connecting rooms. Then he assisted Kari inside.

"You need more ice for that ankle," he said as she leaned heavily against him.

"I know. I was hoping it would be much better by now." She didn't bother taking off her coat, but dropped into the closest chair. "Are you hungry?"

"I could eat," he said, although what he really wanted to do was to dig in to the investigation. "Do you want me to see if they do takeout? That way you don't have to walk on that ankle."

Her face brightened with the possibility. "Oh yes, I would love that."

He crossed over to the information booklet that just about every motel room on the planet had and paged through to find information on local dining. Sure enough, not only did the Apple

Grove restaurant offer takeout, but they included their entire menu in the booklet.

"Here, decide what you want and I'll call it in."

Thirty minutes later he returned with their dinner—grilled salmon and broccoli for Kari and barbequed spareribs for himself. Kari waited until he'd unpacked their meals and taken a seat before she bowed her head to pray. He followed her lead, knowing they had much to be grateful for.

"Dear Lord, thank You for keeping us safe today and for the food You have provided for us. We ask that You continue to guide us on Your chosen path. Amen."

"Amen," Marc echoed in a low tone.

Kari glanced up at him in surprise, and when she smiled, he felt something shift in his chest, her warmth and vulnerability getting to him in a way he'd never experienced before.

But having feelings for his witness wasn't appropriate. For one thing, he needed to stay focused on keeping Kari safe and feelings would only be a distraction.

And even if the trial were over, he didn't do relationships. Hadn't his failed marriage to Jess proven that? She'd promised to love him in sickness and in health, but apparently not in boredom, during the long hours he worked late on a hot case.

This feeling of intimacy, sharing a meal as the snow continued to fall outside the motel window, wouldn't last. Not in the real day-to-day world. This was only an illusion.

He dug in to his meal, enjoying the tangy zip of hot sauce that exploded on his tongue.

"Those look amazing," she said, eyeing his ribs with something akin to envy.

"Do you want to try some?" He gestured to his container. "Help yourself."

She hesitated, then shook her head. "No, thanks, I don't want to risk heartburn—something new since I've discovered I'm expecting."

Yeah, and then there was the fact she was pregnant. Kari had enough going on in her life right now.

They ate in silence for several minutes, lost in their thoughts. Normally, Marc would work as he ate, but he sensed Kari wouldn't appreciate that, so he refrained from reaching for his laptop sitting on the table to his left.

His phone rang, and his gut sank when he recognized Miles's number. "What's wrong?"

"We found the tracking device," Miles informed him. "I'm not surprised you missed it—I almost missed it, too. We stashed it the bottom of a garbage can and dropped your car back at your place."

The initial spurt of fear faded. "Thanks, I'm glad to hear it. At least now I know they can't track us any longer."

"That might not be entirely true, Marc. Is that computer you're carrying around issued by the Feds?"

He glanced at the laptop. "Yeah, so?"

"Mitch and I were talking and we don't think you should use it. The right person could trace the IP address to find you. Especially if you're on an unsecure network."

Marc ground his teeth together in frustration. "Great, that's just great. Why didn't you think of that sooner? You could have brought me a different computer when we swapped rides."

"Hey, don't blame me," Miles said defensively. "Mitch is actually the one who thought about it."

Getting mad wouldn't change anything so he blew out his breath in a resigned sigh. "Okay, I won't use it tonight, but I need a new computer as soon as possible."

"Mitch is actually picking up a new device as we speak. I have to follow up on a new case I've been assigned, but he'll bring it over tonight."

The tightness around his chest eased. "That would be good. I'll give him a call."

"Later, then," Miles said.

He pushed the end button and set the phone aside.

"Your brothers really care about you, don't they?" Kari murmured.

"Yeah, they do." As much as his family drove him crazy at times, he couldn't imagine his life without them. "Mitch is stopping by later."

"I'm glad." She yawned widely, as if suddenly exhausted. "I don't know why I'm so tired. It's not like we did much today."

No, just ran from gunmen in an SUV, not once, but twice, hid in a barn and were now holed up in their third motel room of the day. "Are you finished eating?" She nodded, so he gestured toward the connecting room. "Why don't you stretch out and put your ankle up on pillows. I'll get some ice."

She took a few minutes to stack their discarded containers together in a neat pile before rising to her feet. He helped her hobble into the room, then grabbed the ice bucket and headed outside.

The snow was still coming down, a good inch of accumulation already by his estimation. Maybe he'd catch up on the news and weather while he waited for Mitch to bring the laptop.

Back inside the warm motel room, he swiped

the snow off his shoulders before crossing over to pack some ice in a towel.

Kari was lying on the bed, her left ankle propped up on a pillow. The bruise marring her pale skin looked worse to him, although the swelling was about the same. He gently draped the towel filled with ice over the top of her ankle.

She let out a gasp, and he jerked toward her in alarm. "What? Did I hurt you?"

"No, but I think I just felt the baby move." Her eyes were wide with wonder. "Quick, put your hand here," she said, pressing against the slight swell of her abdomen.

He froze, but couldn't force himself to move closer. "That's great, Kari," he said lamely. "Excuse me, but I have to check the weather." He bolted from the room as if being chased by a rabid dog.

Once he was back in his own room, he felt like a colossal fool. What was wrong with him? Why couldn't he share in something so beautiful?

In a flash he was back in the cold, sterile morgue, identifying Jessica's body, listening as the medical examiner explained that the blow to her head likely knocked her unconscious, so she didn't suffer.

And did he know his wife was three months along in her pregnancy?

The ribs he'd enjoyed earlier threatened to

erupt from his stomach, so he swallowed hard and did his best to push the memories aside.

Kari's miracle of new life had nothing to do with him. A fact he'd do well to remember.

SEVEN

Disappointment surged as Marc disappeared into his room, avoiding her. His refusal to share the thrill of the moment stung, more than it should. Obviously, this was his way of letting her know that while he might be willing to protect her, there wouldn't be anything more between them.

Not even friendship.

Kari slowly rubbed a hand over her belly, hoping the baby would move again. Granted, the books on pregnancy had warned that the fluttering could also be nothing more than gas, but she didn't think so.

There! The fluttering beneath her fingertips came again, and this time she could tell by the way it felt that the movement was from the baby. She continued smoothing her hand over her slightly rounded abdomen, awestruck by the knowledge that she carried a tiny life deep within.

She wondered if the baby was a boy or a girl, but also knew that she didn't want an ultrasound to find out for sure. The sex of the baby one way or the other didn't matter to her; she would love whatever God graced her with. And she wanted the gender of the baby to be a surprise.

She listened to the muted voice of the television coming from Marc's room; the distance separating them felt like miles rather than feet.

Maybe she'd offended him in some way. Feeling her baby move was probably too personal. She had to remember that once she testified at trial, she wouldn't see Marc again.

A muffled thud outside had her jerking upright, her heart hammering in her chest. The gunmen couldn't possibly have found her again.

Then she heard Marc open his door, greeting someone on the other side. She relaxed back, remembering his brother Mitch was bringing over a new laptop.

She strained to listen as they spoke.

"Where are you going to start?"

"I hope to dig into the financial situations of everyone involved in the task force."

"Seriously? Talk about an impossible task."

"I know, but the only other clue we have is the tattoo and so far that's been a dead end."

"What does it look like?"

Kari heard the rustle of paper and realized Marc was showing his brother her drawing.

"Interesting design—you're sure it's a dead end?"

"Nothing popped from the database. I suppose it's possible there could be something local that I'm not aware of."

"A tattoo artist might know something. There's a guy by the name of Jericho Nevis who works downtown in the third ward. Give him a call, see if he can shed some light on the design."

"Thanks, Mitch, I owe you one."

"Nah, you'd do the same for me. Let me know if you need anything more." Kari heard the door open and shut as Mitch left the motel.

She was glad Marc was going to keep working on the tattoo angle. She couldn't help thinking a design that intricate meant something significant.

More muted voices, either the television or Marc talking quietly on the phone, she couldn't be sure which. Slowly, she relaxed, her eyelids growing heavy with fatigue, but when she heard another strange noise her eyes opened in alarm, every muscle in her body going tense. She glanced around the room, but of course nothing seemed out of place.

The fact that the events of the past few days were lingering in her subconscious bothered her. They were safe here so she should be able to relax.

She wished Marc were here, rather than in a different room. Would he think she was overly needy if she asked him to work here for a bit? Maybe, but wasn't it worth feeling foolish if the tradeoff was that she'd get some sleep?

"Marc?" She called his name before she could talk herself out of it.

He materialized in the doorway between their rooms. "Yeah? Something wrong? Are you feeling okay?"

"I'm just—a little on edge. Would you be willing to use your computer in here for a while? I can't seem to relax being in here alone."

He hesitated, but then nodded. "Sure, not a problem." He disappeared momentarily then returned carrying the new laptop. He sat at the small table that was an exact replica of the one in his room, and then sat down and reopened the computer.

"Thank you," she murmured.

"You're safe now, Kari." His eyes were kind and reassuring.

She nodded and allowed her eyes to drift shut.

Amazing how much better she felt, knowing she wasn't alone.

His sandalwood scent intermixed with the sound of his fingers tapping on the keyboard lulled her to sleep.

Marc was far too aware of Kari sleeping just a few feet away. She looked younger, more innocent in repose and he liked the way her hair fanned out on the pillow, her hand cupped protectively over her abdomen. He stood watching her for several minutes before forcing himself to turn away.

This wasn't the appropriate time or place to become aware of a woman. Especially not someone he needed to protect.

He'd called Jericho Nevis, the tattoo artist Mitch referred him to, but the woman who answered the phone said Jericho was busy. Marc left his name and number, but didn't hold out much hope that Jericho would return his call any time soon.

Basic background checks of the task-force members didn't tell him much. He did uncover a few interesting tidbits—the newest agent, Angela Wright, had a younger brother by the name of Warren, who had a juvie record. The record was sealed, and in order to get access to the details, he'd have to use his secure federal access codes, and he wasn't ready to do that yet. Was it possible Angela's brother was involved in something like drugs, guns or gambling? Would she go so far as to set up a series of bank robberies to help get him out of trouble?

He made notes about Warren Wright, but somehow he couldn't see Angela doing something like that. Then again, he couldn't really envision anyone he knew stooping so low.

Detective Steve Young was getting divorced, and Monique Barclay had bad credit. FBI Agent David Hermes was behind on his child-support payments from a divorce that happened several years ago. So far Jason Wu was the only member of the task force, aside from Marc, who didn't have some sort of financial or family issue going on.

Technically, Marc had family issues, too, only he'd managed to keep them under wraps. No one knew that his wife Jessica had been pregnant and that the baby wasn't his. He'd done the DNA testing on his own, outside the investigation. The police hadn't seen a need to do DNA testing, since there was nothing in the car crash that had made them think foul play. Alone in the car, she'd somehow driven straight into a tree. When her drug screen had verified the fact that her blood-alcohol level was above the legal limit, the detectives had closed the case as a DUI without probing any further.

He tapped the pen against the pad of paper, trying to figure out his next steps. His phone rang and he quickly answered it, hoping he hadn't woken Kari.

She shifted a bit, but didn't open her eyes.

"Callahan," he whispered, taking the phone into the other room.

"Mitch, my man, how's it going?" The guy's voice held a hint of an Australian accent.

"Actually, I'm Mitch's brother, Marc. He gave me your number, said you'd be willing to answer a few questions."

There was a long pause, and Marc imagined that Jericho was scowling at the phone. "Depends on the questions," he finally answered with a note of caution.

"Mitch tells me you're the best tattoo artist in the area, and that you might know something about the design of a samurai sword and cobra."

"If you want to know about tattoos, you've come to the right place. Samurai sword designs aren't as popular now as they used to be. Do you have a picture of the tat you can share with me?"

"Sure, I'll text you a copy from my phone and call you right back." Marc missed having his multi-function phone as he performed the laborious task of snapping a picture of Kari's drawing, then texting it to Jericho. He waited a long minute after sending the text to call the tattoo artist back. "Did it come through okay?"

"Sure did. Interesting design, but not my work."

Marc hadn't really expected to get that fortunate. "Do you have an idea of who might do this type of thing? The tattoo was located on the upper front of a man's chest."

"There is a Japanese tattoo artist by the name of Mikio who does many samurai designs. I recommend you start with him first. If he didn't do the design, then he may know who did."

Marc smiled grimly, reaching for a pen. "Tell me where I can find Mikio."

Jericho rattled off the address of Mikio's shop. "I will tell you this—Mikio means 'man like a tree' in Japanese, and he is very tall and very strong. If he thinks you are going to cause trouble, Mikio won't hesitate to defend himself. He has interesting Japanese artifacts in his shop, including several swords."

Marc understood the implied warning. "Thank you, Jericho. I appreciate your help on this."

"Tell Mitch he owes me a favor," Jericho said, then disconnected from the call. Marc wasn't sure if Jericho was serious about collecting on the favor or if that was his idea of a joke.

After heading back into Kari's room, he typed in the address of Mikio's tattoo shop, inwardly groaning when he realized it was located in a pretty rough part of town.

He glanced at his watch. The hour wasn't that late, just seven thirty in the evening. From the information on the website it appeared Mikio's hours were from one in the afternoon until one in the morning.

Should he head down there now? He glanced at Kari, hating the idea of leaving her here alone. But he wasn't about to take her with him, so the only question was, which of his siblings would be willing to come out here to sit with her while he took off for a few hours?

Marc tried Mitch first. "Just got called to the scene of a fire and arson is suspected. I'll be tied up for a while."

Miles was working a series of armed robberies, and Matthew was on duty for the night shift.

He didn't particularly want to call his sister. Maddy was great company, but he needed someone who could manage the potential danger.

Finally, he reached his brother Michael, quickly filling him in on the situation. Michael was a private investigator, and Marc made sure to mention the fact that he should bring his gun.

"If you could get to the Silent Knight Motel as soon as possible, Mike, I'd appreciate it."

"I'd rather go down to the tattoo joint," Mike

muttered. "Tell me what you need and I'll deliver."

He hesitated. "It's not that easy. I'm not sure I even know what I'm looking for. Will you please give me a couple of hours?"

"Yeah, yeah. Okay, I'll meet you in thirty."

Marc disconnected from the call and returned to Kari's room. He stopped abruptly when he noticed she was awake and sitting on the edge of the bed.

"How long did I sleep?" She asked, rubbing her eyes.

"A little over an hour." He drew in a deep breath, knowing she wasn't going to like his plan. "Listen, I need to run a quick errand. My brother Mike is going to come out here to stay with you while I'm gone."

She dropped her hands from her face and frowned. "Call him back and tell him not to come. I'm awake now so I'll just go with you."

"That's not an option. It's too dangerous. For one thing, the tattoo joint happens to be located in a rough neighborhood…"

"I'll stay in the truck," she interrupted.

He shook his head. "No way. A woman sitting alone in that area is an easy target. I can't protect you from inside the building and I also can't afford to be distracted by worrying about your safety."

Her gaze narrowed. "Don't you think I'll be worrying about your safety? Maybe your brother should go with you as backup. I'm sure I'll be fine here alone."

"Not happening." As much as he wouldn't mind having his brother along as reinforcement, he couldn't bring himself to leave her alone. Especially considering the fact she had a badly sprained ankle. If by some chance the black SUV did show up, she'd be a sitting duck.

"So it doesn't matter to you that I'll be worrying?" she persisted. "Stress isn't good for the baby, remember?"

"I'm a trained federal agent and I'll be armed. There's no reason for you to be concerned or stressed. I'll be fine, Kari, and I'll be back as quickly as possible."

She glared at him, clearly not happy. He wasn't sure what else to say. He didn't want to spend the next thirty minutes until Michael arrived arguing with her.

His mind was made up and nothing she could say or do would change it.

"I don't like it," Kari muttered, struggling to her feet. He crossed over and offered his arm. She shook her head, refusing his help as she made her way toward the bathroom. Before he could say anything else, she disappeared behind the door.

He paced as he waited for his brother, trying to think of a nonconfrontational way to approach Mikio. By the time Michael arrived, he still didn't have a great plan.

"Thanks for coming, Mike."

His brother nodded, his gaze sweeping over the room, zeroing in on the open connecting door. "She okay with being left alone with a stranger?"

"Not really. But you're my brother, not a stranger."

"Same difference to her." Michael's serious gaze rested on Marc. "I'll give you two hours. If you're not back here by then, I'm calling for reinforcements."

"Don't call anyone from the FBI or the MPD," Marc warned. "Miles and Mitch both know the situation."

Michael lifted a brow, then nodded. "Okay, family first."

Marc pulled on his winter gear, double-checked to make sure his weapon was locked and loaded before heading outside. The snow had stopped and the clouds had dissipated. The reflection from the moon glittered like diamonds on the freshly fallen snow.

He brushed the snow off the truck, then jumped behind the wheel and headed toward Milwaukee's north side. The truck was too nice for the area, but his brother's car was also new, so there wasn't a good alternative.

Finding the tattoo shop wasn't difficult, but Marc drove around the place twice before choosing a place to park. He wanted to be well positioned for a quick getaway, just in case.

He hunched his shoulders against the cold and crossed the street. There was a wide window to the right of the doorway, displaying Mikio's name and several Japanese designs, mostly dragons. There was also a small neon sign in blue and green that read Tattoos located on the left side of the door.

As he came closer, his pulse leaped when he saw a samurai design in the window. It wasn't the same one that Kari had drawn, but there were enough similarities that made Marc think he'd come to the right place.

But would Mikio admit the design was his? From what he knew about tattoo artists, they liked to boast about their work, especially since new customers were often gained by referrals.

If Mikio was paying attention to the news, he'd know Jamison was under arrest and heading to trial. Kari's name as a key witness had also been leaked to the media. For all he knew, Mikio would deny having anything to do with the design.

Marc took a deep breath, pulled Kari's design

out of his pocket and entered the tattoo shop. The snow must be keeping people away, because the place was empty except for a tiny Asian woman with every centimeter of her skin covered in ink standing behind the counter, and a large burly guy who was also covered in tattoos. The man looked at Marc with suspicion as he approached.

He smiled and tried to look nonthreatening. "Hi, you must be Mikio, my friend Jericho told me all about you."

Mikio continued staring, his eyes flat and seemingly devoid of all emotion. "Who wants to know?" he finally asked.

"I'm Marc Callahan, and I heard you do incredible samurai designs." He carefully set Kari's drawing on the top of the counter. "I am curious to know if this is one of yours?"

"Why?" Mikio asked with a scowl.

"I'm not here to cause trouble," Marc said. "I would just like to know if this is one of your designs. From what I can see, it seems as if you pride yourself on being original."

"It is mine," Mikio said in a gravelly voice.

Marc relaxed a bit. "Will you tell me about the man who received this tattoo? Did he come alone or was he with someone?"

Mikio moved to the side, but then suddenly held a glittering curved sword in his hand, the tip pressing against Marc's sternum.

Marc froze. Even through his heavy winter coat, he could feel the tip of the blade and knew it could easily pierce the fabric and penetrate straight into his heart.

Maybe he should have had Mike come with him as backup. He had a bad feeling that if he even tried to draw his gun, Mikio would skewer him like a shish kebab.

EIGHT

The seconds ticked by with excruciating slowness. Marc forced himself to stay where he was, sensing that backing down from Mikio wasn't the right way to go.

"Mikio means 'man like a tree,'" Marc said, breaking the silence. "I have great respect for you and your work. I don't want to cause trouble—I only want to know if the man who received this tattoo was here alone or with someone else."

"He came with two others," the Japanese woman said in a bored tone. "Earlier in the year, maybe February or March? It was winter. They came several weeks in a row, as these designs cannot be completed in one sitting."

Marc didn't take his eyes off Mikio. "Thank you. Is there any chance you have their names?"

"No names," Mikio said. "Cash only."

"I see. Would you be willing to show me the designs the other men received?"

Mikio must have made some sort of hidden

gesture to the woman, because she pushed away from the counter with a sigh and opened up a picture album. "These are the other two designs."

Marc was loath to move closer, but then Mikio backed up a step, giving him a little room. He angled his head to see the designs. Belatedly, he realized having Kari here would have come in handy since he couldn't draw and doubted he'd be able to describe the designs in a way that she could sketch them.

"Very impressive," he said with admiration. "The detail is exquisite. May I take a picture?"

The sword didn't move away from the center of his chest, but Mikio gave a slight nod. "One hundred dollars."

Marc carefully pulled out his wallet and peeled off five twenty-dollar bills. The woman scooped up the money. He used his cell phone and snapped a quick picture.

"Thank you." He pocketed the cell phone then took a step back. The tip of the sword moved away from his chest, and he tried not to show his relief.

"You will be sure to tell Jericho I have been most helpful," Mikio said.

"Of course." Marc decided he wasn't going to argue the fact that being most helpful cost him a hundred bucks. "Thank you again."

As he turned and walked toward the door, he prepared to react if Mikio came rushing after him brandishing the sword. When he made it outside unscathed, he hurried to the truck. When he slid into the driver's seat and started the engine, he realized the meeting with Mikio had taken less than ten minutes.

Ten minutes that had taken ten years off his life.

Marc drove back to the motel, hoping that the photos of the tattoos had been worth the hundred dollars he'd paid for them.

They desperately needed a clue that might lead them to Jamison's accomplices.

Kari soaked in the tub, trying to relax for the sake of her baby. She refused to think about what dangers Marc might be facing.

Okay, maybe a truer statement would be that she tried not to dwell on what Marc would be facing. How dangerous could going to a tattoo shop be?

She pulled on her clothes and combed her hair with her fingers before emerging from the bathroom, feeling physically refreshed. Clean clothes would be nice, but truthfully she was grateful for what she had.

When she saw a stranger hovering in the doorway between the connecting rooms, she stopped and leaned against the bathroom doorjamb. The man had the same dark hair as Marc, but was leaner in build, and maybe a little shorter. He wore his hair long enough to brush the back of his collar and had the same brilliant green eyes as Marc, which she found interesting as Miles and Mitch both had blue eyes.

She crossed her arms over her chest. "You must be Michael, the private investigator."

Michael didn't smile, but did tip his head in a curt nod. "Are you all right? Do you need anything?"

These Callahan men were all good-looking and polite. But even from the tiny bit of interaction she had with them, they were all very different. Miles the flirt, Mitch the laid-back one. So far, Michael's serious expressionless demeanor was the most like Marc's.

"Of course I'm all right. Why wouldn't I be?" She hobbled over to the bed. "When do you expect Marc back?"

"Within the next hour and a half."

That long? She grimaced and reminded herself to breathe slow and deep, no stress. "All right."

"You want me to look at your ankle?"

"No, thanks."

Michael nodded, then disappeared back inside Marc's room. She stretched out and propped her foot up on pillows, not that she thought elevating it really helped much.

She closed her eyes and tried to fall asleep. There was no sound in the room next door, not from the television or the computer. Perfect for sleeping.

Or not.

Several minutes later, the low rumble of a truck engine reached her ears. She sat up and flipped on the lamp. Was that Marc returning already? Was the fact that he was back so soon a good thing or not?

Sure enough, the door of the motel room opened and then shut. Since sleep was impossible now, she swung herself upright and hopped over to the door.

"Any problems?" Michael asked.

Marc set a bag on the table next to the computer, glanced over at her, then shook his head. "No. It cost me a little money, that's all."

Michael grunted then grabbed his jacket. "Let me know if you need anything."

"I will. Thanks again for coming out."

"No problem." Marc's brother drew on his coat then let himself out without saying anything more.

"Talkative guy," she said.

That made Marc smirk. "Yeah, Mike isn't much for chitchat."

"I noticed." She watched as he pulled out his phone and crossed over to her. "What did you find out?"

"Jamison got his tattoo at the same time two others did. These are their designs." He showed her the photograph on his phone. "I know it's small, but do you think you can draw them for me? I stopped and picked up a drawing pad and pencils at the store on my way back."

She peered at the side-by-side images on the phone. "I can draw them, but it would be better if they were blown up bigger."

"Well, there's no need to start tonight. You can draw them in the morning."

"I'm awake now," she pointed out. "Might as well make good use of my time. What will you do with the sketch?"

"Get it into the database, see if we can get any hits."

She gnawed her lower lip. "But I thought we couldn't use the FBI computer system."

He nodded. "I'm thinking of making a quick stop at my place, at least long enough to check these additional tattoos. I need to know if they match anyone we've arrested in the past."

She frowned. "You're not going to leave me behind again, are you?"

"That depends. But let's work on getting the sketches done first, okay?"

"All right." She slid the drawing pad out of the bag, admiring the thick paper. He'd also purchased a large package of pencils in a variety of colors. Eager to get started, she took a seat at the table, opening the pencils and spilling them out on the table. "Wouldn't it be easier to send the images to the computer?"

"I thought of that, but the images are a little blurry. I think your sketches will work better."

"Okay." She didn't mind doing them. In fact, she was glad to be able to help.

Marc fiddled with the phone, setting it up so she could see the images. She opened the sketchbook, picked up a black pencil and began to draw.

Everything in the room around her faded away, even Marc. Immersing herself into her art, she created the first image, adding color since he'd purchased the pencils.

When she finally looked up, she was surprised to see that Marc was watching her intently. She blushed when she realized he'd probably been staring at her the entire hour that it had taken her to complete the drawing.

Odd that she hadn't noticed. Normally, she didn't like to have people watching while she worked. But for some reason, she wasn't as self-conscious around Marc.

"What do you think?" She turned the sketch so he could see what she'd done.

"Incredible." The admiration in his tone made her blush. "I know I said this before, but you're very talented."

"Obviously, you haven't spent enough time around art," she teased. She flipped over the page and picked up the black pencil again.

Forty-five minutes later she tossed down the pencil with a sigh. There was a dull ache between her shoulders from sitting so long and her vision was beginning to blur, but she'd finished them. "Here you go. I hope these additional tattoo designs help find the men who assisted in setting up the bank robberies."

Marc stood and came over to take the sketchbook, setting it aside. "You look exhausted. Can you stand or should I carry you?"

"I can stand." At least she thought she could. She planted her hands on the table and levered herself upright, keeping her weight off her injured ankle.

Marc muttered something under his breath and then she was up and in his arms for the second time that day. He carried her into her room and gently set her down on the bed.

His face was dangerously close for several long heartbeats before her arms dropped away, allowing him to step back.

"Good night," he murmured, turning off the light as he left the room.

"Good night." She rested back against the pillow, Marc's sandalwood scent surrounding her, providing a comfort that had eluded her earlier.

Moments before she succumbed to sleep, she realized that she was depending on Agent Marc Callahan a little too much. Not just to keep her safe from harm. But for emotional support, as well.

A weakness she could not afford.

Sleep didn't come easy to Marc. He kept thinking about how close he'd come to kissing Kari. Completely inappropriate thoughts, because not only was she his witness and his responsibility, but she was pregnant with another man's child.

Kari's pregnancy kept reminding him of Jessica's secret. Granted Kari's situation was different than Jessica's decision to have an affair, but he couldn't deny the deep-seated urge to stay far away from having anything to do with Kari's unborn child.

So why had he almost kissed her?

Because he'd been alone too long in the two years since Jessica's death. Even as the excuse filtered through his mind, he knew he was lying to himself.

Truth was, he liked and admired Kari. Her strength, her resilience, her determination to do whatever was necessary for the sake of her baby. She was the opposite of Jessica in so many ways.

Kari was the last thing Marc thought about when he finally fell asleep and she was also the first person he thought about when he woke up the following morning. A fact that made him grumpy.

After a quick shower, he yanked on his clothes while planning his next steps. He didn't want to use the new computer to log in to the FBI database, which left only one alternative. If he used the desktop computer he had at home, the leak within the task force could only trace the access back to his house. And he figured that once that happened, he and Kari would be long gone.

It could work. If there wasn't someone keeping a close eye on his place. Which he had to believe there was. All he needed was a way to get in without being seen.

His condo was on the tenth floor of a building that overlooked Lake Michigan and the parking garage was located underground. The truck he'd borrowed from Mitch couldn't be connected to him, so if they could get inside, taking the elevator up to his place wouldn't be difficult.

A surge of adrenaline pulsed through his

bloodstream. If he pulled this off, the risk was minimal, at least in the grand scheme of things.

He heard movement from Kari's room, indicating she was up. A glance at his watch told him that it was seven thirty in the morning. Plenty of time to eat breakfast before heading downtown.

When he poked his head through the doorway, he noticed her bathroom door was closed. Since she needed time to get ready, he decided to make coffee, using the tiny coffeemaker supplied by the motel.

Marc found himself staring at Kari's drawings, wondering about the three men who'd gone in together to Mikio's tattoo shop. Terrance Jamison had been one of the men, but he needed to know about the other two men. There was no guarantee that they were Jamison's accomplices, but it was a good place to start.

Hopefully, they'd get a hit in the federal crime database.

"Good morning." Kari's soft voice broke into his troubled thoughts and when he glanced up at her, he was struck once again by how pretty she was. Her brown hair was still damp, framing her face and touching her shoulders. Her cheeks were flushed and her dark eyes were wide and bright, fringed with long lashes. She didn't wear an ounce of makeup and he never realized how much he liked her natural beauty.

"Good morning." His voice came out husky and he cleared his throat awkwardly as he rose to his feet. "How's the ankle?"

"A little better," she said, glancing down at her foot. "It doesn't hurt as much today and I think the swelling is finally going down."

"I'm glad to hear it." He picked up her sketchbook. "Are you hungry? The restaurant across the street serves breakfast."

"Very." She smoothed her hand over her stomach, and he almost asked if she could feel the baby moving again.

Not his business, he reminded himself.

"Let's go. We'll need to take everything with us. We're not going to stay here for another day."

"Where are we going?" she asked, taking the sketchbook from his hand and scooping up the pencils and then tucking them into a plastic bag. Marc shut the computer, then tucked it under his arm. "I mean, after breakfast. You mentioned going to your place to get access to the FBI database?"

"Yeah, that's still the plan. I'll explain over breakfast."

Kari nodded.

He opened the door, letting in a cold blast of air. "Wait here. It's too slippery."

After storing the laptop behind the driver's seat, he started the engine and turned the heat on high as he brushed the snow from the windshield. When he was finished, he went back inside for Kari.

"Hang on to my arm," he said. "I don't want you to fall and twist the other ankle."

"I hope I'm not that clumsy," she muttered, but he noticed she held on tight while taking careful steps to get over to the truck. There were no running boards for her to use, so once again he hoisted her into the seat.

The parking lot of the restaurant had been salted and plowed, so the going was easier there. Once they were settled into a booth and had placed their orders, he filled Kari in on his plan.

"You really think someone might be watching your condo?" she asked when he'd finished. She took a sip of her decaf coffee, eyeing him over the rim.

"It's what I would do," he responded.

"Shouldn't you ask one of your brothers to help?"

"Not this time. The truck is our best disguise since they have no idea what we're driving. We have a good chance of getting into the parking garage without being noticed, especially if you crouch down in the seat."

"They might still recognize you."

He shrugged. "I'll stop and pick up a hat and sunglasses. We'll be fine."

The waitress arrived with a large tray of food. He sat back so she could set down the plates as she warned them they were hot. She refilled their coffee, and then left.

Marc glanced at Kari and reached his hand across the table. "Let's pray," he suggested.

Her smile lit up her entire face, and she took his hand, then bent her head. "Dear Lord, we thank You for this food we are about to eat. We also thank You for keeping us safe in Your care. Please continue to guide us on Your chosen path. Amen."

"Amen," Marc echoed, reluctantly releasing her hand. He couldn't deny a sense of peace that washed over him as soon as they finished their prayer, and he felt ashamed that he'd allowed himself to stray from his faith.

His mother, his whole family, would be disappointed if they knew the truth. And he was grateful for Kari for reminding him about what was really important.

The food tasted great, but they didn't linger too long. He paid the bill in cash and they both used the restrooms before heading back outside.

The sky was partly cloudy, but there was enough sunlight to provide a good excuse for wearing sunglasses. He pulled into the first drugstore he found, bought what he needed then returned to the truck.

"Ready?" he asked, glancing over at Kari.

"Sure. When do I need to crouch down on the floor?"

"I'll let you know when we're within a few miles," he promised. He didn't like the idea of her crouching down on the floor without the ability to wear a seat belt, but it wouldn't be for long.

When they were a mile from his usual exit, he looked over at her. "I need you to get down now."

She quickly unlatched the seat belt and slid down onto the floor. The truck was so large, and she was so tiny, she fit just right.

Wearing a knit hat and sunglasses, Marc kept a keen eye out for any sign of a vehicle that seemed out of place. Since Kari had smashed their windshield, he couldn't be sure if they'd replaced the broken window or switched cars.

He didn't see anything out of place until he turned the corner to approach the entrance to the parking structure located halfway down the street. A black SUV with tinted windows was parked on the opposite side of the road.

A coincidence? Or were the gunmen inside, watching?

With his heart pounding, he slowed down, knowing that he had to act as if he belonged there. Just before he turned into the parking garage a large semitruck with the name of a food supplier painted on the trailer came lumbering down the road from the opposite way, momentarily blocking him from view.

Taking the opportunity, he clicked the remote on his key chain to gain access to the parking garage. The door opened with excruciating slowness, but soon he was inside. He glanced in the rearview mirror, grateful to see that the semi-truck was still out on the street. He quickly hit the remote, closing the door behind them.

He drove in and parked next to his car located in his designated parking spot and shut off the engine. He knew his neighbor traveled for business, so Garrett's truck would be okay there for a while. As much as he wanted to believe they were safe, he couldn't deny the fact that there was only one way out of the underground garage and that was going out the same way they'd come in.

Driving right past the SUV with tinted windows. He could only hope and pray that either the vehicle was long gone by then or that they'd manage to get away safely.

NINE

Admittedly curious about Marc's home, Kari followed him into the elevator located straight across from where he'd parked. The interior was lined with floor-to-ceiling mirrors, and she winced when she saw her reflection standing next to him.

Even wearing the knit cap over his dark hair, he looked tall, handsome and strong. His square jaw was covered in a five o'clock shadow since there were no razors at the motel, but somehow that only made him more attractive. She felt short and chunky beside him in her secondhand winter coat, leggings and rounded abdomen. Her hair looked dull and limp thanks to not having a brush. The only saving grace was her dark eyes.

Wait a minute, what was she thinking? That she wanted Marc to think of her as pretty? As a woman he might one day be interested in? Talk about letting her imagination run amuck—he'd already made it clear that there was nothing personal between them. That he was only doing his job in protecting her as a witness, keeping her safe.

And she was grateful to him for that. For everything he'd done for her since the safe house had been breached. He'd rescued her from the tree house and shielded her from harm on multiple occasions. To expect anything more would be incredibly selfish.

She pushed the ridiculous longing away, watching as the elevator rose up one level at a time. When they reached the tenth floor, Marc stepped aside, giving room for her to walk out first. Their footsteps were soundless on the plush carpet as they approached the door to the left of the elevator. Marc used his key to unlock the door, then stepped back to allow her to go inside first.

When she crossed the threshold, she was oddly disappointed to see the place looked like something out of a fancy magazine. Lots of beige, black, white, glass and chrome, nothing seemingly out of place.

No color? How in the world did he live without color?

As if sensing her disappointment, Marc grimaced. "I know it looks a little impersonal, but I don't spend a lot of time here. I'm usually at work or spending the weekend with my family."

She nodded, wondering what his mother thought about the stark decor. Not that his choices were any of her concern.

"Don't use any lights and stay away from the windows," he cautioned as he took off his coat and tossed it over a chair. "We don't want to alert anyone that we're inside."

"Okay." She removed her coat, too, draping it over his. "Do you have a home office?"

"This way." He led the way down a short hall to the first door on the right. The office was just as austere as the rest of the living quarters. The only difference was that he had a framed photograph of his family sitting on his desk. Curious, she moved closer to get a better view.

An older couple stood in the center of the photo, with Marc and his brothers and sister surrounding them. They were all smiling broadly for the camera, except she noticed Michael's smile wasn't as open and friendly as the rest. She wondered why his expression seemed a bit guarded.

"My parents' thirtieth wedding anniversary," Marc murmured, coming up beside her. "Taken about three years before my father was killed in the line of duty."

She touched the frame with the pads of her fingers, wishing she could meet everyone in

Marc's family. "I'm sorry for your loss. You must miss him very much."

"Yeah." He hesitated, as if he might say something more, but simply moved away and turned on his computer. She took the sketchbook out of the bag and handed it to him. He placed her drawing on the combo printer and scanner and then sat down behind the desk to go to work.

Kari tore her gaze from the family photograph and tried to think of something to do to occupy her time. She wandered back into the living room, knowing she couldn't go near the windows, but still enjoying the amazing view of Lake Michigan.

As beautiful as it was, she couldn't imagine living here. It was too cold, too impersonal. Too downtown. If there had been any lingering fantasies about getting together with Marc on a personal level when the trial was over, seeing the way he lived in the fancy condo squashed them like a bug.

Her vision of a home was very different. Her dream was to provide a warm, cozy place to raise her baby, complete with a small grassy backyard and a swing set. Her furniture wouldn't match, but that wouldn't matter as long as it was comfortable and childproof.

Just the thought of tiny handprints smudging

the glass coffee table made her cringe. Definitely not her type of place.

Which meant Marc wasn't her type of man.

Taking a deep, steadying breath, she headed back into the office. Marc was seated behind the desk, scowling at the computer screen. The only comfy chair she could see was an overstuffed black leather recliner in the corner. She picked up the sketchbook and curled up in the seat.

While Marc searched the FBI database, she drew a picture of a sunrise over the lake, with tiny sailboats bobbing on the water and seagulls swooping down to pluck fish from the blue depths. She used the colored pencils to add vibrant oranges and reds to the sky and a mixture of blues and greens for the water.

As usual, she became lost in her art, hearing the water sloshing against the shore, the call of the birds as they dove for food. When she finished the sketch she became aware of Marc's intense gaze.

"I love watching you work."

She blushed and averted her eyes, hoping he wouldn't notice the effect he had on her. "Did you find anything?"

"Not yet. Show me your picture."

She turned the sketchbook so he could see, feeling self-conscious about her decision to overemphasize the colors.

"Beautiful," he said, his green gaze full of appreciation. "Do you work in other mediums?"

"Sure, when I have time. I love oil paints and was using the second bedroom in my home for a studio but had to pack everything away to make room for the baby." She turned the sketchbook around and opened to another blank page.

She was halfway through another drawing of Marc when he jumped up from his seat, startling her. "I found it!"

"What? One of the tattoos?" She tossed the pad aside and rose to her feet. Her ankle was beginning to hurt again, but she tried to hide it as she gingerly made her way over to see the computer screen.

"Does this guy look familiar to you?" he asked.

She stared at the mug shot of a man with brown greasy hair and a bushy beard staring blankly at the camera. She took her time before shaking her head. "No, I'm afraid not. Who is he?"

"His name is Tomas Lee and he has this tattoo on his chest as a distinguishing mark." He showed her a second photograph of one of the designs she'd sketched from the picture on his phone.

It was an identical match.

"Do you think he's one of them? Jamison's accomplices?"

"It's the best lead we have so far." Marc grinned and hit a button on the computer. Within seconds his printer whirled to life and began spitting out pages.

His excitement was contagious. This guy could turn out to be a real clue. "If we find this Tomas Lee dude, will I still have to testify?"

Marc's smile faded. "Yes, Kari. I'm sorry, but you'll still need to testify."

She pursed her lips together and nodded. Deep down she knew there was no escaping the inevitable so she wasn't sure why she kept pushing the issue. It was just that every day that went by brought her another step closer to seeing Jamison again. And even though he couldn't hurt her anymore, she still remembered the ice in his gaze, the gun he'd pointed at her chest.

There had not been a single doubt in her mind that he would have killed her. The same way he'd murdered the bystander who'd tried to take him down. The gunshot had been so loud, and there had been so much blood.

She shivered and rubbed her hands over her arms. Marc crossed over to stand beside her. "It will be okay."

"I know."

He put his arm around her and gave her a

hug. She rested her cheek against his chest and wished more than anything that this nightmare would end so she could go back to her normal, dull, everyday life.

When his arms tightened around her, pulling her close, she turned more fully into the embrace, wrapping her arms around his waist and tipping her head back to look at him. She intended to assure him she was all right, but then his head dipped toward hers as if he intended to kiss her.

And she couldn't stop herself from meeting him halfway, sighing with pleasure when his mouth gently took possession of hers.

His kiss was potent, causing all rational thought to instantly evaporate. In that moment, Kari realized just how different this chemistry was from what she'd experienced with Vince.

It was more, so much more.

Marc wasn't sure how the kiss happened, but once he'd tasted Kari, he found it difficult to stop. She was so sweet, so innocent.

It took every bit of willpower he possessed to break off the kiss, and even then he had trouble drawing breath into his lungs. He didn't let her go right away, unwilling to cause her to misstep and hurt her ankle again.

She finally loosened her grip and pushed

away, limping heavily as she made her way back to the overstuffed chair. It had been the only item of furniture that he'd taken from the home he'd shared with Jessica.

The chair had once been his father's.

Marc rubbed the back of his neck, mentally kicking himself for kissing Kari. What was wrong with him? He'd never crossed the line with a witness before.

And he absolutely shouldn't have done it now.

Yet at the same time, he couldn't bring himself to apologize. Because he wasn't sorry for kissing her. In fact, he wanted to kiss her again.

Get a grip, he warned himself.

"We need to get ready to go," he said, breaking the uncomfortable silence.

"I know," she said in a breathless voice.

Marc turned and walked over to the printer to gather the information he'd found on Tomas Lee and the details related to Angela's brother's juvie record. It hadn't contained much, just some minor vandalism when the kid was thirteen. He slid the paperwork into a folder, then frowned when he realized the black folder containing the bit of intel he'd pulled together on his father's murder was missing from the corner of the desk where he thought he'd left it.

Had he misplaced it? He opened every desk drawer, looking for the folder, but without success. There were plenty of manila folders that he used for work, but the black folder had contained all his personal notes, the autopsy report and the police report related to the night his father was gunned down.

"What's wrong?" Kari asked.

"I misplaced a file," he muttered, going through the entire office in a methodical fashion. Maybe the cleaning lady had moved it? Although he'd been using the same service for the past year and they'd never touched any of his things before.

Twenty minutes later, he collapsed back in his chair, forced to admit it was gone. Someone must have stolen it.

But who? And why?

It wasn't like many people had access to his condo. The cleaning lady had a key as did his mother. No one else. Not even his brothers.

Of course, his brothers could probably get the key from his mom if they really wanted to. But none of them would come in when he wasn't here. And they surely wouldn't take the black file folder from his desk, even if they saw it.

He hadn't told anyone in his family about the fact that he'd begun his own investigation into his father's death. At first, he'd convinced his family to let the police detectives work the case.

After all, they would have expected the same consideration if the roles had been reversed.

But when the weeks turned into months, Marc knew it was time to take matters into his own hands.

"Do you want me to help?" Kari asked. She rose out of her seat and hobbled to the desk. "What are you looking for?"

"A black file," he said. "But it's not here."

"Black, huh?" A smile tugged at the corner of her mouth and he was forced to avert his gaze, trying hard not to think about kissing her again. "Do you have something against green?"

He blinked. "Green?"

"Or blue, or red or yellow…" She waved a hand in the air. "There's a whole spectrum of colors to choose from and you bought black folders? Really? Who does that?"

"I—um…" He sighed and shrugged, feeling a bit like a fool. "I guess I haven't cared much about that sort of thing, not since my wife died."

She winced as if his words had slapped her. "I'm sorry… I didn't know. I have a bad habit of sticking my nose where it doesn't belong."

"Don't worry about it." Strangely enough, he didn't want Kari to feel bad for him. His pain over his wife's death was centered around his feelings of guilt intermixed with anger and resentment. Guilt, because he knew that he hadn't been the husband she'd wanted and deserved. Anger and resentment over the way she'd chosen to cheat on him to get his attention.

The ultimate betrayal, though, was to allow herself to become pregnant by the man she'd run to. For weeks after he'd discovered her pregnancy, he'd wondered if she'd planned to leave him the night that she'd crashed. If she'd gotten pregnant on purpose, so he couldn't ask her to stay, to try to work things out.

But sitting here now, looking at Kari, he acknowledged the fact that even if Jessica hadn't died the night when she'd driven her car into a tree, their marriage wouldn't have survived. He'd thought he'd loved her, but in retrospect, it wasn't the same sort of deep, abiding love he'd witnessed between his parents.

What did that say about him? He didn't like thinking about it because it hurt too much.

"I'm sorry, Marc," she said again.

"Don't be. You had no way of knowing she died two years ago. And if you want to know the truth, my father's murder is what's bothering me the most. The black folder contained my notes and other documents related to his death."

"Okay, then we'll find it." Kari leaned against the desk, easing her weight off her ankle. "Should I look in the kitchen?"

"No. I only worked on that file here in my

office." He rose to his feet. "Could be that I accidently took it to work with other stuff. It's not important now. We have what we came for. Tomas Lee was only held in jail for a few months then released on parole. I have his last known address here, so we can swing by and check things out."

"All right," Kari agreed. "While we're here, do you want to pick up anything else?"

"Why not? Sit down. I'll pack a duffel bag of extra clothes. I have some sweatpants and shirts for you, too."

"I wouldn't turn down a change of clothes," Kari said with a smile.

He realized he should have taken her in with him when he'd picked up the knit hat and sunglasses. "We'll stop at the drugstore on the way so you can grab anything else you might need."

"That would be great. I'd love a hairbrush."

He nodded. He left the office and ducked into his bedroom to quickly throw some things together. He added shampoo, toothpaste and a couple of spare toothbrushes. Anything else Kari needed could be grabbed later.

As long as he was in his room, he double-checked the drawers on his nightstand, just to be sure he hadn't brought the folder in here. But of course it wasn't anywhere to be found.

The missing folder nagged at him, even

though he knew he couldn't afford the distraction from the case he was currently working on. He slung the strap of his duffel bag over his shoulder and returned to his office, where Kari was waiting.

His lips curved in a grin when he saw that she'd taped her colorful drawing of the lakefront to the front of his desk, so that it was the first thing anyone noticed as they walked into the room. "Nice."

She shrugged and came over to meet him. "You need a bit of color in your life, Marc," she said in a low voice. "Both your wife and your dad are in a better place with God. And they'd both want you to move on with your life, no matter how painful or difficult that might be."

His throat swelled, choking him with emotion, making it impossible to speak. He nodded, then held out his arm, silently inviting her to lean on him as they made their way out of the condo.

He wasn't convinced Jessica was with God, but he was absolutely sure his father was. Max Callahan had lived a good Christian life, instilling a sense of community service into his children. His dad had put his life on the line more than once to protect the innocent.

Until the night he was shot down in cold blood.

Kari tightened her fingers on his arm, causing him to look down at her. "Are you okay?" she asked gently.

The invisible binds around his throat loosened. "Yes, I'm fine. Thanks."

Her smile was tentative, as if she didn't quite believe him.

When they reached the door, he paused. "We're going to do the same routine on the way out of here, okay? Unfortunately, you'll need to crouch down on the floor again."

"Understood," she agreed.

He wondered if leaving within an hour of arriving would look suspicious to anyone who might be watching, then shrugged it off. The SUV with tinted windows might not even belong to the gunmen.

Kari opened the door leading into the hallway of the condo. It was still empty, not unusual for this time of the day, when most of the occupants were at work.

They rode the elevator down to the parking garage in silence, and he was glad they didn't run into anyone else as they returned to the truck. He lifted Kari inside, his heart lurching a bit when she smiled at him and murmured, "Thanks."

He slid behind the wheel, then waited until she was settled back on the floor. After pulling on the knit hat and the shades, he put the gearshift into Reverse and backed out of the spot.

The remote control on his key ring opened the garage door. Marc gripped the steering wheel tightly, hoping the black SUV was gone.

It wasn't.

Keeping his gaze averted from the vehicle parked across the street, he drove up the ramp and turned right, taking the opposite direction away from the SUV.

"Are we clear?" Kari asked.

One glance at the rearview mirror made his gut clench with worry. The SUV with tinted windows had pulled away from the curb and appeared to be following them. He wanted to believe it was nothing more than a coincidence, but then he noticed the small dent in the roof of the vehicle, right above the windshield.

Was it possible the dent was from the heavy-duty scraper Kari had hurled at them?

TEN

"No. We're not clear," Marc said in a voice that vibrated with tension. "The SUV is behind us."

Kari curled herself into a tighter ball, closed her eyes and prayed.

Dear Lord, keep us safe in Your care!

Her body swayed when Marc turned a corner. He didn't pick up his speed; in fact, he turned on the radio to a rock and roll station and bobbed his head to the beat.

What in the world was he doing? He wasn't acting at all like an FBI agent.

Maybe that was the point?

Her body swayed again, and the momentum of the truck increased. It was disconcerting to be huddled down here unable to see where they were going.

"You can get up now," Marc said, turning down the radio.

"Really? They're not behind us anymore?" Kari began to uncurl herself from the floor.

"No, they turned around. Either they weren't the gunmen or they went back to watch the condo."

It took a few minutes for the words to sink in to her brain. "We got away? The disguise worked?"

The corners of his mouth lifted in a smile. "Yep."

She crawled into the passenger-side seat and snapped the seat belt in place. She didn't want Marc to know just how vulnerable she'd felt on the floor, knowing he wouldn't have asked her to do such a thing if there had been another way.

"Now what?" Kari glanced through her window, looking at the now-familiar landscape. They were headed west, leaving Lake Michigan behind.

"First we'll find a drugstore," Marc said. He glanced at her but the sunglasses hid the expression in his eyes. "Then I'd like to check out the last known address listed for Tomas Lee."

She was thrilled at the idea of getting some toiletries, but inwardly grimaced when she remembered she didn't have any money. Of course Marc would lend her some, but she didn't like the idea of using his money on personal items.

Fifteen minutes later, Marc took an exit off the interstate and headed for a well-known drugstore chain. It wasn't the same place he'd stopped earlier and she knew he'd made that decision on purpose.

When he threw the gearshift into Park, she unlatched her seat belt. Before she could ask him for cash, he pulled out his wallet and handed her several crisp twenty-dollar bills.

"Thank you," she murmured, sliding the bills into the pocket of her sweatshirt. "You can stay here. I won't be long."

He nodded, as if sensing she didn't particularly want an audience to buy personal items and other toiletries.

Kari quickly found everything she needed and made sure to mentally tally the items in her basket before stepping into line at the checkout counter.

The woman behind the counter didn't look twice at her purchases. Kari paid the bill and then limped outside. She found herself scanning the parking lot, double-checking to make sure the black SUV wasn't anywhere in sight.

Marc jumped out of the truck and came to meet her halfway. "Find everything? Do you need more money?"

"No, I'm good." She kept the bag clutched close to her chest, too embarrassed at the thought of him seeing what she'd purchased. He opened the truck door for her and once again lifted her into the seat.

"I'm not a fan of this truck. It's a pain to get in and out of," she muttered, tucking a strand of hair behind her ear.

"It wouldn't be so bad if your ankle wasn't hurt," he said with a smile.

"I'm pretty sure that I wouldn't be able to get inside once I'm a few weeks further along, even with a good ankle."

His gaze dropped to her belly, then jerked back up to meet hers. "You're right. I hadn't thought of that." He shut the door and walked around to the driver's side.

It bothered Kari the way Marc seemed to retreat a bit every time she reminded him of her pregnancy and she wondered again about the kiss they'd shared. Why had he kissed her if her condition bothered him? Was it possible he'd completely forgotten she was expecting?

Now that the immediate threat of danger was over, she couldn't help reliving their brief but sizzling kiss.

Marc's embrace made a mockery of the intimacy she'd shared with Vince. Making her wish all over again that she hadn't allowed him to sway her from her beliefs.

Then again, she couldn't regret the end result of being pregnant.

"Something wrong?" Marc asked, breaking in to her thoughts. "Are you feeling all right?"

"I'm feeling fine," she assured him.

"Rest up a bit," he suggested. "The address I'm looking for is a good twenty minutes from here."

She nodded and closed her eyes, but unfortunately she could still see a clear image of Marc in her mind. The intensity of his gaze moments before he captured her mouth with his.

The fluttering in her abdomen returned, making her smile. She slid her hand beneath her coat and pressed it against her stomach, enjoying the experience of feeling the baby move.

Her son or daughter was what was important, not pining over a devastatingly handsome FBI agent. A man who she knew full well wouldn't have looked twice at her under normal circumstances.

He was aware of her only because of their forced proximity. And the same was true for her.

Four more days till the trial. Surely, she could find a way to hold on to what little remained of her common sense for that long?

Marc wondered what Kari was thinking, but forced himself to concentrate on finding the place Tomas Lee called home. Unfortunately, the address was located in a rough part of town, and he didn't like exposing Kari to that environment.

Once he'd pinpointed the place, he could always come back later on his own. Hopefully, one of his brother's wouldn't mind sitting with her for a while.

It took longer than he'd anticipated to find the house, and when he finally identified the structure that corresponded to the address listed on the parole sheet, he frowned when he saw several broken windows, a giant hole in the front porch and a yellow notice taped to the door.

Condemned.

Tomas Lee might have lived there once, but clearly no one was living there now. At least, not legally.

Marc drove slowly past the house, then swung around the block to make another pass. There was a slim possibility that Tomas was still inside, but considering the frigid temperatures and the ramshackle building, he didn't think that was a likely scenario.

"Is that the place we're looking for?" Kari asked.

"Yeah, that's it." He glanced over and gestured to the manila folder between them. "Check to see if there's a number for his parole officer."

She flipped open the file. He made another circle around the block, then drove back toward the highway.

"There is a number listed here. Do you want me to call it?"

"Yeah, if you wouldn't mind. Just plug in the numbers and then give me the phone."

She did as he asked, handing the phone to him the moment there was ringing on the other end of the line. Someone picked up on the fifth ring. "Officer Clayton Hughes."

"Officer Hughes, my name is Marc Callahan and I'm with the FBI. I'm looking for some information on a former parole of yours, a guy by the name of Tomas Lee."

"Lee, Lee…" Hughes muttered. "Oh yeah, I remember him. Did a short stint for armed robbery. Why do the Feds want him? Is he in trouble again?"

"Do you remember him having a samurai tattoo on his chest?" Marc asked, avoiding the parole officer's question. "A rather large design with a warrior, a sword and mask."

"Nah, I don't pay attention to that stuff. As long as he follows the rules of his probation, he can do what he likes."

"What's the last known address you have on file for him?" Marc asked. "The one on Central Street?"

"Just a minute." There was a thunk as Hughes put down the phone, then the sound of shuffling papers. Almost a full minute later, Hughes picked up the phone. "Nah, that's not what we have. We have the one listed on Appletree.

Twenty-Third and Appletree, the number on the building is 2358."

Marc glanced at Kari, repeating the address out loud. "Twenty-Third and Appletree, building number 2358. Is there an apartment number, too?"

"Apartment 204. What has Lee done, anyway? Must be bad if the Feds want him."

"I appreciate your assistance," Marc said. "I'm afraid I can't go into details about the case I'm investigating."

"Wait a minute, I have a right to know what's going on," Officer Hughes protested. "What if this jerk comes back here with a gun or something?"

"You should absolutely consider him to be armed and dangerous," Marc responded in a calm voice. The parole officer was putting on a big act, but the truth was, all parole officers dealt with dangerous ex-cons every day. Many of whom had been convicted of worse crimes than armed robbery. "If you see him call for backup."

"Hrmph."

"Thanks again, Officer Hughes." Marc disconnected from the call then handed the phone back to Kari, repeating the address he'd been given.

"I've written it down," she answered.

Marc nodded and headed to the opposite side

of the city, closer, he noted, to the area where Mikio's tattoo shop was located.

He felt certain he was on the right track. Tomas Lee must have been one of the men who'd accompanied Jamison to get their samurai tattoos. And if that was the case, then it wasn't much of a stretch to believe the two men had worked together on the series of bank robberies.

Of course, actual proof would be nice. Something other than similar tattoos obtained several months before the first bank was hit.

"I'm not sure you should approach Tomas Lee alone," Kari said. "It would be better for you to have one of your brothers go with you, since he's considered armed and dangerous."

"Right now, I just want to drive by the apartment building, get an idea of where it's situated and what else might be around." Marc thought it was sweet the way she worried about him. Unnecessary, but sweet. "And don't forget I'm armed, too."

"I know, but still…" Her voice trailed off.

He kept his attention on the traffic as he navigated the truck toward Appletree, making sure to keep an eye out for any sign of the black SUV. He couldn't afford to let his guard down, and forced himself to consider all the possibilities.

If there were a link between the gunmen and someone within the task force, they could easily run the license plates of the truck. Garrett Rolland's name wouldn't be readily associated with the Callahans, but if they cared enough to dig into Garrett's background, they'd learn that Mitch's buddy happened to be stationed in the military overseas in Afghanistan. Which in turn would raise some red flags about who was driving his truck.

He drummed his fingers on the edge of the steering wheel. He didn't like it. Not one bit. Maybe he should think about picking up some other vehicle.

On the other hand, how many black SUVs were there in the city? Lots. So he might be worrying over nothing.

He kept track of the street signs, going down to Twenty-Third Street. Then he headed south to Appletree Lane. The apartment building wasn't in great shape, although not nearly as bad as the condemned house Lee had lived in previously. There was only a single window that was lined with Christmas lights, and he didn't see any Christmas trees through any of the windows, either. Maybe because it was daytime.

He drove past the building, trying to think of a way to get inside without tipping off Tomas Lee that he was coming. There was an intercom system, but as he drove by he watched someone walk into the building without using a key.

The lack of security would work in Marc's favor. But as much as he wanted to go inside now, he didn't particularly want to risk exposing Kari to danger.

He swung his gaze around, taking note of the businesses located around the apartment building. A small Mexican restaurant, a tavern, an old video store that was boarded up and a liquor store.

"I really wish you'd call your brothers," Kari said again.

"I'll try, but they have work to do, too. I can't drag them away from their own cases. But for now, we'll find a place to stop for lunch, then look for another motel to spend the night."

Her expression mirrored her relief. "Good, I'm glad you're going to wait until later."

Not that much later, but no need to bring up that point now. If he was working alone, he wouldn't bother stopping for lunch, but Kari needed to eat, for her sake as well as for the baby's.

"What are you in the mood for?" he asked, heading back toward the west side of the city.

"Doesn't have to be anything big and fancy. Soup and a sandwich works well enough."

He pulled into a small sandwich place that he liked, knowing there would be plenty to choose from on the menu. They headed inside and ordered their meal.

Kari chose a booth along the far wall, and he set down the tray then claimed the seat facing the door. He reached over again to take her hand, then bowed his head in deference to her heartfelt prayer.

It was strange the way he fell back into the habit of praying before meals, much the way his parents had taught him. Jessica had gone through the motions, but she hadn't really believed in the power of faith, not the way Kari clearly did.

"Your turn next time," Kari said with a grin, releasing his hand.

He was tempted to take her hand back, missing the warmth and softness of her skin, but managed to refrain. "Sure."

For several moments they ate in silence, enjoying the simple meal. The tomato soup was excellent, warming him from the inside out.

"Have you ever considered going to art school?" he asked. "Your talent is wasted at the bank."

Her smile evaporated. "I took some graphic-design classes at the technical school, but that's all. As much as I'd love to make money from drawing or painting, I really need a regular paycheck coming in, especially now."

He nodded; he could certainly understand where she was coming from. Soon she'd have another mouth to feed. "I'm sure saving up money for tuition isn't easy."

"No, it's not. I had some money set aside, but after my mom died, I used it to pay for her funeral."

Her matter-of-fact statement hit him square in the solar plexus. Obviously, her mother didn't have any life insurance and the thought of Kari planning and paying for her mom's funeral all by herself made him feel terrible. "I'm sorry you were put in that position."

"Yeah, well the waitresses at the diner where she worked took up a little collection, too. It wasn't much, but every little bit helped. I was just starting to rebuild my nest egg when I met Vince." She wrinkled her nose. "You know how that ended."

Marc wanted to punch Vince Ackerman in the gut for knocking Kari down after she'd just gotten herself back on track. A surge of protectiveness caught him off guard and he knew he was getting too personally involved in Kari's well-being. She was smart, pretty, talented, and deserved so much more.

Which reminded him, he hadn't heard anything about the sketch of Vince he'd given to

Miles. "Yeah. I hope when we find him, he still has some of the cash he stole from you."

She lifted her hand palm up in a *whatever* gesture, as if she didn't hold out much hope for that. "What about you? When did you go to the academy?"

"As soon as I finished my four-year criminal-justice degree. The timing was perfect—they'd just opened up several positions and I was glad to be chosen. I guess I've been with them for almost four years now."

"You mentioned Miles works as a police detective and that Michael is a private investigator. Is everyone in your family involved in law enforcement in some way or another?"

"Yeah, Mitch is an arson investigator and Matthew is training to be a K9 cop with his new partner, Duke. My sister, Madison, is a lawyer with the DA's office."

"Your parents must have been so proud of all their children receiving college degrees." Her voice held a hint of longing, but he couldn't tell if it was because of his family, their college educations or both.

"We're very blessed," he agreed. He finished his sandwich and crumpled up the wrapper, waiting for Kari to finish.

Since she was still eating, he decided to try his brothers, starting with Miles. When he got his brother's voice mail, he left a message asking if he'd gotten any leads on Vince, before disconnecting from the call.

Kari's eyes never left his face as he worked his way through his brother's numbers, leaving brief messages with each one. He didn't bother bugging his sister and dragging Maddy into danger wasn't an option, either.

"Now what?" Kari asked, dropping her napkin on the tray and pushing it away. "Do we go find a motel?"

"That would be the logical thing to do," he admitted.

"Do I hear a *but* on the end of that?" she asked wryly.

"You could drop me off at the apartment building, and drive around while I have a chat with Tomas. We both have phones, so I'd be able to call you when I'm ready to be picked up."

She regarded him with a steady gaze. "Don't you think it would be better to wait for one of your brothers to call back?"

"Maybe, but I haven't heard back yet, and don't want to wait. I'm armed and I doubt Tomas will try to shoot me in broad daylight."

"I'm not sure about this," she said, biting her lower lip nervously. "I don't like the thought of you going in alone."

"Kari, I need to do this. I promise I'm trained

for these types of situations. For all we know, Tomas might not even be home."

"Okay," she reluctantly agreed.

He tossed out their garbage and set the tray on top of the others already stacked above the trash can. Kari put her hand in the crook of his arm, still favoring her left ankle. At least her injury wouldn't prevent her from driving the truck.

The ride back to Appletree Lane didn't take long. When they were a few blocks away, he parked the truck and switched spots with Kari. She had to adjust the driver's seat up as far as it could go in order to reach the gas pedal.

"This thing is ridiculous," she muttered.

"You'll be fine." At least, he hoped so. Leaving Kari in the truck didn't sit well, but it was better than leaving her all alone. "If anything happens, take the cash I gave you, find a hotel and call my brothers. They'll take care of you."

She shot him a withering glare. "But nothing is going to happen to you, right?"

"Right. See that opening in front of the boarded-up video store? Drop me off there."

Kari pulled over as he asked. He tucked his phone in his pocket and slid out of the truck. "Don't go too far. I'll be in touch."

"Be careful."

He nodded and slammed the passenger-side door behind him. He waited until Kari pulled away from the curb to head down the street toward the apartment building.

The lock on the main door was broken, so he was able to get inside easily enough. He bypassed the tiny elevator in favor of the stairs. When he reached the second floor, he headed down toward number 204, which happened to be right next to the stairwell.

He listened at the door, trying to gauge if anyone was home. There wasn't any sound coming from inside. Either Tomas was sleeping or he was gone.

Marc lifted his fist and rapped sharply on the door. He waited, listening intently, but still nothing. For kicks, he tried the door handle and to his surprise it wasn't locked.

"Hello?" He pushed the door open, but kept his back against the wall. He held his weapon ready as he edged farther into the room.

The apartment had been tossed like a pro. Everything had been thoroughly searched, sofa cushions slit open and drawers dumped on the floor.

It didn't take long to ascertain the apartment was empty. But as Marc looked around the interior, he couldn't help wondering what they'd been searching for.

And if they'd found it.

ELEVEN

Gripping the steering wheel, Kari drove slowly, navigating the seemingly too-narrow city streets. She'd never driven a vehicle this massive and found it difficult to judge where she was on the road. She actually winced as she went past some areas where there were cars parked on either side of the road.

Amazingly, she didn't hit anything.

Two blocks west of the apartment building, she found a large open area alongside the road that was a perfect place for her to park. She made a circle, going past the apartment building one more time in case Tomas Lee wasn't home and Marc happened to be outside waiting for her.

When there was no sign of him. Her pulse kicked up a notch. Obviously, Tomas was home and she had no idea how their conversation would go. Marc was armed and trained as an FBI agent, but that didn't mean he was infallible.

He was human and would bleed just like anyone else if injured.

She went two blocks west, pulled into an empty space along the side of the road and shifted the truck into Park. Then she took a deep breath and reminded herself that getting upset wasn't good for the baby.

Her fingers and toes were beginning to get cold when her phone rang. She was so startled she dropped it. After picking it up, she answered, "Hello? Marc?"

"Come pick me up," he said in a brusque tone.

"On my way." She disconnected from the call and carefully pulled away from the curb. Making the loop back toward the apartment building didn't take long, and when she noticed the grim expression on his face, she knew something was wrong.

Kari climbed over the console, giving Marc room to get behind the wheel. Once she had her seat belt latched, she turned to face him.

"What happened?"

Marc pulled away from the curb and put some distance between them and the apartment building. When they were safely out of the area, he let out a heavy sigh.

"Tomas Lee wasn't home, but someone had searched his place. It's a total wreck." He gestured to the phone sitting between them. "We'll need to call it in, but without giving our names. We need to remain anonymous."

"Searched for what?" she asked, trying to understand this latest setback. "And where is Tomas?" She was relieved he wasn't dead, like the officer who'd been sitting outside her safe house. But the news still didn't bode well for Tomas.

"I'm not sure, unless someone was looking for the money from the robberies." Marc shrugged. "I don't understand it, either, and I can't help but think Tomas might be in danger. Maybe from the third guy who'd been with them when they got their tattoos? All I can do is speculate at this point."

She picked up the phone with shaking fingers and dialed 911.

"What's your emergency?"

Kari gave her the details, but when the dispatcher pressed for more, she lost her patience. "Just send the police." Kari disconnected from the call and then quickly powered down the phone, knowing the dispatcher would attempt to call her back.

"Thanks for making the call," Marc said.

"Do you think we had the wrong apartment?" She wanted to believe they'd made a mistake, that their one clue hadn't just led them to a dead end. "Maybe Tomas Lee doesn't really live there any longer."

"I saw some mail on the floor addressed to Lee and postmarked four days ago. I think it's his place, although I guess we can't know for sure that he's living there alone."

"If he has a roommate, it could be the apartment was trashed because of something that person did."

Marc grimaced and shook his head. "Seems like a pretty strong coincidence to me. We suspect that Lee is involved in the bank robberies. What are the chances that the ransacking of the apartment isn't related? I'm not buying it. There's definitely something odd going on here."

She hated to admit he was right. That would be one incredible coincidence. "Well, we know Jamison wasn't the one who trashed the place."

"You're right about that," Marc agreed. "Which means someone else is attempting to cover up their participation in this. Someone who is going to extreme lengths to keep their secret. Now that I've seen what happened in Lee's apartment, I'm starting to get a little worried about Jamison."

"Jamison? But he's safe in jail, isn't he?" Even as she said the words, she knew the answer. Of course not. No one was ever safe in prison. "You really think it's possible that someone could be bribed into killing Jamison while he's in custody?"

"Yeah. Unfortunately, I do."

"But why?" Her stomach knotted at the thought of someone paying money to have Jamison killed. As much as she dreaded the thought of testifying at trial, she didn't want to get out of it by having the guy murdered.

"That's the part I can't quite figure out," Marc admitted. "There were several attempts to kill you, to keep you from testifying, which would cause us to drop the charges against Jamison. But why go after Lee? And if someone does want to try to silence Lee permanently, why not just kill Jamison, too, and leave you out of it?"

She had no idea. "What should we do now?"

"I'm not sure. I can't call my boss if that puts us in danger, but I feel like there are still several puzzle pieces missing. At the moment, I can't figure out if Jamison's life is in jeopardy or not."

"It wouldn't hurt for him to have extra protection, regardless, right?" she pointed out. "Maybe we could leave another anonymous tip?"

"Not sure a tip like that would be taken seriously. I could ask Miles to request additional security."

She frowned. "But they'd know that you put him up to that, wouldn't they?"

"Someone was already following him," he reminded her. "I'm sure they know that I've been in touch with my family. So yeah, they'll know the request actually came from me. But I can't think of another way to get the word out to the jail administration."

She couldn't think of another way, either. "Do you want me to call Miles?"

"Not yet. I already left him and my other brothers messages, so I have to assume they're busy. Hopefully, one of them will call me back sooner than later."

"Okay." She stared out the windshield, wondering about the person who'd searched Lee's apartment. A thought occurred to her, and she reached over to grasp Marc's arm. "Marc, what if Jamison finds out about Tomas Lee's apartment being searched? Couldn't that information be used as leverage to encourage him to confess as to who else might be involved?"

He glanced over at her, his gaze full of admiration. "Now you're starting to think like a cop," he said with approval. "You're right—that's a good idea."

The warmth in his green eyes caused her to blush. "Obviously, I've been hanging out with you for too long," she teased.

His grin widened. "Touché," he said. "The only problem is that I'm not sure who can get that information to Jamison. My brother is a police detective, but I doubt anyone will give him access to talk to a federal prisoner. And I can't trust the members on the task force, either."

"Then we're back to talking to your boss. I know that you don't trust the members of the task force, but do you honestly think your boss is the leak? Couldn't you trust him with at least this bit of information?"

"Maybe, but I refuse to use our new phones to contact him." Marc tapped his fingers on the top of the steering wheel. "Let me think about it. Maybe a brief call from a pay phone would work."

"Do they even have pay phones anymore?" she asked. She couldn't remember the last time she'd seen one. Then again, with the evolution and availability of cell phones she hadn't really needed to look, either.

"Probably not many. But we should keep an eye out just in case. They're most likely going to be at gas stations or convenience stores."

The phone in Marc's pocket rang, diverting her attention from searching for a pay phone. He took the phone out of his pocket and handed it to her. "Put it on speaker."

She hit the button and held the device between them.

"Marc? What's going on? I'm still investigating a new homicide. Why do you need someone to stay with Kari again?"

"I don't need that anymore. I already checked out the apartment leased by Tomas Lee. Unfortunately, he wasn't there, and his place has been trashed from top to bottom."

"Who's Tomas Lee? One of the accomplices involved in the bank robberies?" Miles asked.

"Yeah. He has a similar tattoo on his chest, in the same spot as Jamison's. There were three men who all received their tattoos at the same time earlier this year. I found Tomas Lee in the criminal database."

Miles let out a low whistle. "That's not good news."

"No, it's not," Marc agreed. "We made an anonymous call to 911 with Kari's phone to send the police out there. But I need your help. We think there is something going on between the bank robbers. Lee and Jamison could both be in danger. I think it's important to heighten the security around him, get him out of the general population."

"Yeah, I agree. I'll do my best, but you know very well I don't have any authority in this case."

"I know, but tell them anyway. I'll keep looking for a pay phone to call my boss."

"Wait a minute, I know where there's a pay phone. Hang on a sec." Miles set down his phone and Kari could hear voices and paper rustling in the background. "Here it is—there's a pay phone at the gas station on the corner of Captain and Hillside."

"How do you know that?" Marc asked, executing a U-turn to head in the opposite direction from where they were headed.

"There was a stalker case we worked on and we were able to figure out that the woman was doing her own phone calls from the pay phone there, claiming they were from her ex."

Kari's mouth dropped open. "Really? She made it up?"

"Yeah, although honestly that doesn't happen often," Miles admitted. "One of the detectives staked out the pay phone and then watched her make the call."

"Unbelievable," she murmured.

"Okay, thanks, Miles. I'll use that pay phone to call my boss to request added security on Jamison."

"Sounds good. Oh, by the way, I have interesting news about the drawing of that guy you gave me."

"Vince Ackerman?" Marc asked, meeting her gaze briefly before turning his attention back to the road. "What did you find out?"

"We believe he's a scam artist who goes by several different aliases. One of them is Victor

Arrowsmith, who allegedly scammed almost ten grand from a woman in Chicago. There are a couple of other complaints against him, too. Unfortunately, we haven't found him yet."

Kari dropped her chin to her chest and closed her eyes. She knew she shouldn't feel so humiliated by being taken in by a crook, but she did. How was it possible she'd allowed herself to be so naive?

"Kari, don't," Marc said in a low voice. "It's not your fault. He's a professional crook and has obviously done this several times before."

She lifted her head, belatedly realizing the conversation between Miles and Marc had ended. After dropping the phone in the cup holder, she folded her arms over her chest. "I know. But that doesn't really make me feel any better."

"Just stay focused on the gift he gave you," Marc suggested. "Your baby needs you."

Kari drew in a quick breath. This was the first time Marc had ever initiated a positive comment about her pregnancy. Oh, he'd said a few things before, but only after she'd broached the subject.

Maybe she was reading too much into his comment, but after that heated kiss they'd shared, she couldn't help thinking that maybe Marc had finally accepted her as she was, pregnancy and all.

* * *

As much as Marc wanted Vince Ackerman, or whatever his name was, to pay for his crimes, he hated seeing Kari so upset. Especially when her only mistake was trusting the wrong man.

Marc wished he weren't driving so that he could take her in to his arms again. Not that he should even think about kissing her. No matter how much he wanted to.

"You're right," Kari agreed. "My baby is my top priority. Well, that and testifying of course."

"Glad to hear it." He glanced at her, knowing deep in his bones that she'd be an excellent mother. Someone who would always put the needs of others before her own.

Very different from Jess. Although, to be honest, it's possible his wife could have changed once the baby was born.

"Aren't we supposed to be heading toward Captain and Hillside?" Kari asked.

He reined in his scattered thoughts. "Yes, we are." He turned at the next intersection, taking the most direct route to the pay phone Miles had mentioned. As he drove, Marc tried to think of the best way to approach his boss.

Special Agent in Charge Evan White wasn't going to be happy to hear from him. In fact, Marc feared his job might be on the line if he didn't follow his boss's orders. Somehow, he had to make him understand the seriousness of the threat against Kari and the need to remain off the grid until the day of the trial.

The call would have to be short to avoid being traced. They'd still be able to figure out where he'd made the call from, but by the time that happened, he and Kari would be long gone.

"There it is," Kari said, breaking into his thoughts.

"I see it." He pulled into the gas station, then jockeyed the truck around so that he could use the phone and still make a quick getaway. "I'm going to keep the engine running, okay?"

She nodded, her hands twisting in her lap as if she were nervous.

He flashed a reassuring smile, dug several coins out of his pocket and then jumped out of the truck. After feeding the money into the machine, he quickly dialed his boss.

"FBI," Evan answered.

Marc took a deep breath. "It's Callahan. Someone is trying to kill our witness."

"Where have you been?" Evan shouted. "I want you to report to my office immediately!"

"Not going to happen." When Evan started to sputter again, Marc interrupted, "Listen carefully, there have been three separate attempts to kill Kari. They traced my car and my brother has been followed, as well. I believe one of Jamison's accomplices is a man named Tomas Lee." He rattled off the address, hoping that his boss was taking notes. "Lee's apartment was ransacked. You need to get more protection on Jamison and convince him to cooperate. Tell Jamison about the break-in at Lee's apartment. Maybe the news will convince him to start talking."

"Report to my office and bring the witness," Evan repeated. "We'll find a way to keep her safe."

Marc ground his teeth together in frustration. "No. I'm sorry, but I believe someone on the task force is dirty. There's no other logical explanation for how the safe house was compromised in the first place, not to mention the way my vehicle was tracked. Only someone with police resources could do something like that."

His boss swore. "I need you to work the investigation, Callahan. We'll get someone else to babysit the witness."

Marc scowled at the phone, glad Evan couldn't see his facial expression. No way in the world was he handing Kari off to someone else, except maybe to one of his brothers. He wouldn't trust anyone else to keep her safe. "I am working the investigation. I just gave you the name of a possible accomplice, Tomas Lee."

"I need to be able to reach you," Evan said. "Can I call you back at this number?"

"No, this is a pay phone." Marc glanced at his watch, realizing he'd already talked for longer than he'd planned. "I'll keep in touch, but I'll only call you and only in your office."

"When?" Evan demanded.

"Soon."

"If you don't call me every eight hours with an update, you can kiss your job goodbye."

"Understood." Marc hung up the phone before his boss could go at him again. He had no doubt that Evan meant what he'd said about losing his job. FBI agents didn't get very far up the career ladder if they refused to obey orders.

But keeping Kari and her baby safe were far more important.

The pay phone rang loudly, and Marc knew that it was probably Evan attempting to call him back. Marc turned his back and jogged over to the truck. He quickly climbed in behind the wheel.

He'd only call his boss back if or when he had new information to share. And not before.

Because right now, he and Kari were better off alone.

TWELVE

When she'd watched Marc talk to his boss, his grim expression and the way he'd hung up the receiver with more force than was necessary convinced Kari the conversation hadn't gone very well.

She hated knowing he was likely in trouble because of her. Well, not because of her but rather the situation she'd found herself in. The men who'd tried to kill her were the real bad guys.

And Marc Callahan was one of the good ones.

She averted her gaze, hoping her growing feelings for him weren't clearly reflected on her face. Marc might have kissed her, but she knew better than to expect anything to come of their brief embrace.

This was the worst possible time to fall for a man. Especially a guy like Marc, who could have his pick of any woman on the planet.

Why on earth would he want someone like

her? No college degree, a mundane job as a bank teller and pregnant with another man's child.

Yeah, she was a real prize all right. Not.

Okay, now she was just feeling sorry for herself. Blame it on the hormones. She pulled herself together and forced a smile. "Where are we headed?"

"We need another motel, preferably someplace far away from the pay phone and not very expensive," Marc said. "My cash reserves are running low."

"I think there's a place near the café where I used to work," she told him. "It's one of those Holiday America chains. I don't know why I didn't think of it sooner."

"Not sure it's a good idea to be close to where you once worked," Marc said. "But I know there's another one on the opposite side of town, so we'll head there."

The idea of anyone digging so deep into her background that they knew the name of every place she'd ever worked was beyond creepy. If her mother hadn't passed away last year, Kari had no doubt that she would have been in danger, too.

Her stomach rumbled with hunger and she hoped it wasn't loud enough for Marc to hear. But the man had ears like a bat, because he quickly turned toward her.

"You're hungry. I should have realized it was beyond dinnertime."

"I'm fine. Let's just get to the motel. We can pick up something once we're settled."

"All right." He made several twists and turns as he drove through traffic, obviously doing his part to make it difficult for anyone to follow them.

Did he ever get tired of it? Not necessarily eluding the bad guys, since this probably didn't happen very often. But always being on alert? Ready for anything? She remembered how he'd answered her call on the first ring the night her safe house had been breached. As if he normally slept with one eye open and one ear listing for the phone.

And for the first time, she wondered what would have happened if she hadn't gotten in touch with Marc that night. If she'd called Detective Monique Barclay instead. Would she have been astute enough to keep her alive? Or would she already be dead?

She shivered, knowing it wasn't smart to play the what-if game. Especially when Marc had answered the phone and kept her safe.

"How about I pick up a couple of pizzas?" he offered, breaking in to her thoughts. "We'll take them with us to the hotel. That way, we can eat while I work."

Her stomach growled again, making her blush. "Sounds good to me."

Less than an hour later, they were settled into a Holiday America hotel with two pizzas, both loaded with the works. The pepperoni and cheese smelled delicious, and waiting until Marc had carried everything inside wasn't easy.

Finally, he dropped onto the chair beside her. He took her hand in his and bowed his head. "Dear Lord, thank You for providing this food for us to eat. We also thank You for keeping us safe in Your care, and we hope You continue to guide us on Your chosen path. Amen."

"Amen," Kari echoed, touched by the way Marc had taken the initiative to pray. "You remembered," she said as she opened the pizza box. She'd only been teasing him at breakfast about how it was his turn to say grace, but he'd taken her seriously.

"Yeah, I remembered." He made sure she had two pieces in front of her before he helped himself to one. "Why do you think I suggested we eat here where we could be alone?"

She chuckled, and took a large bite of her slice, enjoying the spicy tang of pepperoni. "Chicken."

"Yep, that's me." He grinned, then dug in to his meal. For several long minutes, they didn't say anything, content to focus on their meal.

When she'd finished three slices, she pushed

the pizza away with a groan. "I can't keep eating like this, or I won't fit into any of my clothes."

"You don't even look pregnant," Marc protested. "I'm sure you'll be fine."

She smiled. "I won't be fine, not if I keep eating like this. My doctor made a point of warning me not to gain too much weight."

His gaze went serious. "When's your next doctor's appointment?"

She had to think back; it seemed like months rather than days since she'd been home. "I think it's a few days before Christmas. Why?"

Marc didn't say anything for several seconds. "The trial is scheduled the first Monday in December and we're fairly certain we can wrap it up in a week."

"I was hoping I could go home after I'm finished testifying," she said with a sigh. "You said I'd only be on the stand a day or two at the most."

"That's the plan," he agreed. He stared down at his pizza, as if he couldn't look her in the eye. "But there is a small problem," he added.

She frowned. "What kind of problem?"

"I'm not sure you'll be safe at home, even after the trial is finished." He lifted his gaze and her stomach clenched at the resignation reflected there.

"Why wouldn't I be safe?" She honestly didn't

understand his thought process. "Once Jamison is convicted, there would be no reason to hurt me."

"Maybe not, but are you willing to take that chance?"

She crumpled a napkin in her fist, resisting the urge to throw it at him. It wasn't as if any of this was his fault. "What are you suggesting, Marc? That I stay in hiding until your task force finds a way to track down and arrest Jamison's accomplices?"

"I think you should consider going into witness protection," Marc said. "Starting over with a new name in a new town with a new career."

Her mouth dropped open in shock. Then she surged to her feet, fury radiating through her entire body. "You've been planning this all along," she accused, unable to keep her tone steady and calm. She clenched her hands into fists. "Why are you just telling me this now? What about my life? I'm just supposed to give up the few friends I have and go somewhere else? Raise my baby among strangers?"

"Kari, please…"

"No! Don't say anything more. I can't talk about this right now." She swung away from the table, putting so much weight on her sore ankle that tears sprang to her eyes. She blinked in an effort to keep them from falling as she made her way through the connecting door to her own room.

Taking satisfaction from slamming the door loudly behind her.

Marc dropped his head into his hands, knowing he messed that up but good.

Yeah, he should have mentioned witness protection before now. Early on, he hadn't broached the topic because he felt certain Jamison would break down and tell them who he worked with. Once they had everyone in custody, there would be no reason to worry about Kari's safety. She could go back to her normal life, planning for her new family.

But then the safe house was breached. And the black SUV had shot at them, twice. Was likely still searching for them.

Being in danger changed things.

He firmly believed Tomas Lee was one of Jamison's coconspirators. Especially after seeing the way his apartment had been ransacked. All they needed to do was find him.

But it was the identity of the third man that concerned Marc the most. Especially if he had connections within the task force. Someone with a law-enforcement background could extract revenge on Kari even after the trial was over, making her death look like an accident.

Over the past few days, the possibility of Kari needing to go into witness protection became real. Especially after he'd seen what had been done to Lee's apartment.

Blurting the truth about her future hadn't been the smartest move he'd ever made, however.

He needed to apologize, but she'd made it clear she didn't want to talk to him. Her anger was understandable; he didn't particularly want Kari to go into witness protection, either.

Her plight wasn't his fault, but he still felt responsible. He was the one in charge of the task force, which meant finding the leak was his responsibility.

Marc rose to his feet and began cleaning up the mess from their lunch. There was almost half a pizza left over, so he shoved it into the small fridge and tossed everything else in the garbage.

Setting his computer aside, he reviewed the information he'd printed out on Tomas Lee. But it wasn't easy to concentrate; instead he kept listening for Kari.

When he'd read the same paragraph three times, he gave up. He strode over to the door between their rooms. It was closed tight and there was no handle on his side, so he knocked.

"Kari? Are you all right?"

Silence.

Was she ignoring him? Or had she fallen asleep?

"Will you please talk to me?" Normally, he was always able to bury himself in his work, ignoring any and all personal problems. Wasn't that what he'd done with Jess? But somehow, he couldn't stand knowing that Kari was upset with him.

Hadn't she said that stress wasn't good for the baby?

He took a deep breath, intending to try one last time, when he heard the click of the lock. The door abruptly swung open and his chest tightened when he realized she'd been crying.

"I'm sorry," he rasped. "I should have mentioned the possibility of witness protection before now. I didn't mean to upset you."

She snorted and turned away to limp back toward the bed. "Yeah, because leaving your entire life behind to start over with a bunch of strangers is something you'd do without hesitation."

Her sarcasm made him wince. The very idea of leaving his family behind was incomprehensible. He followed her into the room. "You're right, I wouldn't be very happy about leaving my family behind."

"Face it, you wouldn't leave your family at

all," she corrected. "You'd figure out some other way to get what was needed."

He couldn't deny her allegation. "You're right."

"Of course I'm right. And just because my mother is gone, doesn't mean I don't have ties to the community."

"I know." He sat down in the chair across from her. "I'm sorry." He'd apologized more to Kari in the short time they'd been together than he'd ever done with Jess.

Maybe he should have done more of that, earlier in their marriage.

"There has to be a way to get to the truth," she said, avoiding his gaze. "If we can figure out who Jamison was working with, I wouldn't have to go."

"Agreed. I promise you, I'll continue working the case, even after the trial is over." He knew his caseload wouldn't make that an easy promise to fulfill, but he'd use every spare moment he had to keep going. "But I think we're getting a little ahead of ourselves, planning for the worst-case scenario." He added, "Could be that Jamison will spill his guts sooner rather than later. Especially if he finds out that Lee's apartment has been trashed."

"Maybe." She didn't sound convinced. Not too surprising, since he hadn't managed to convince himself, either. Nothing about this case was going as planned. There had to be something he was missing.

But what?

Why wouldn't Jamison talk? What game was he playing? How would keeping silent work to his advantage?

He wished he knew.

"Do you think I can spend Christmas at home, before I have to leave?" she asked.

His stomach knotted, wishing he could assure her she could enjoy a nice Christmas celebration.

With him? And the rest of the Callahan gang?

The idea had a strange appeal. He liked Kari… a lot, more than he should. The exhilarating kiss they'd shared was imbedded in his memory.

Wait a minute, what was he thinking? His family would assume things were serious if he brought Kari home with him. And he'd never hear the end of it from his mother, Nan and the rest of his siblings. Especially Maddy.

On the other hand, the idea of seeing Kari again, once the trial was over, wouldn't go away. At first, her pregnancy had reminded him of everything he'd lost, but now, he found himself wanting to be there for her.

Not that she'd given any indication that she felt the same way.

She was staring at him waiting for his response, so he did his best to reassure her. "Try not to worry about it now," he said softly. "It's better if we take it one day at a time. We have to get through the trial before we can think about what will happen afterward. And I suspect that once Jamison is found guilty, he'll be more likely to cooperate with us, maybe in exchange for a lighter sentence."

She grimaced. "I'll try." She rubbed her chest.

"What's wrong? Do you feel sick or something?"

"Heartburn from the pizza," she muttered. "Having pepperoni for lunch seemed like a good idea at the time, but now, not so much."

A grin tugged at his mouth. "I might have some antacids in my bag."

"Really?" Her eyes brightened. "Enough to spare? That would be great."

"Of course." Relieved that she seemed to have forgiven him, at least for the moment, he hurried into his room to find the antacids. He suffered from heartburn occasionally, as well, and was glad he had something to help make her feel better.

"Here you go," he said, spilling two flavored tablets in the palm of her hand.

"Can I see the bottle?"

"Sure." He held it out so she could read the label.

"Calcium, that's good for both me and the

baby." She popped them in her mouth, chewed, then scowled. "Too bad they taste like chalk."

"Unfortunately, they do. But if this is a side effect of being pregnant, you may as well get used to it," Marc said wryly. "Just remember it could be worse."

"Yeah, thanks."

He watched her for a moment, struck again by her wholesome beauty. Maybe it was partially because she was pregnant, but her cheeks held a soft glow.

"I guess I'd better get back to work," he said, rising reluctantly to his feet. "Let me know if you need anything."

"I'm fine," she assured him. "The antacids should do the trick."

He nodded, sticking his hands into his pockets to resist the urge to cross over, take her in his arms and kiss her.

Opening up his laptop, he began searching for more information on Tomas Lee. But there wasn't much out there—it seemed that Lee had been keeping a low profile, at least until he'd teamed up with Jamison to do the bank robberies.

Marc stared at the tattoo designs. The men had gone together back in February or March to get their matching tattoos. Did that mean that they'd been planning the bank robberies even back then? The way they'd struck so many different banks in such a short period of time, less than two weeks, made Marc think that they'd done a fair amount of leg work prior to the main event.

Which meant that whoever was involved inside the task force had been in on the planning, as well.

He went back to the members of the task force. Detective Steve Young's wife had filed for divorce in November of the previous year. Detective Monique Barclay's credit score had also taken a hit about the same time. Agent David Hermes credit wasn't that great, either, thanks to his late child-support payments.

Marc figured he could put Agent Angela Wright and Detective Jason Wu at the bottom of the list for now, focusing his efforts on the other three with financial issues.

His phone rang, jarring him from his thoughts. He pulled out the phone, recognizing his brother Miles's number. "Hey, Miles, what's up?"

"I have news about Tomas Lee," his brother said.

Marc mentally braced himself, expecting the worst. "Oh yeah? What?"

"We found his body in a back alley, not too far from his apartment. He had a gunshot wound in his right temple."

Marc let out a heavy sigh. "Homicide?"

"My instincts say yes, but the ME hasn't ruled out suicide," his brother replied. "Tomas Lee was right-handed and there are traces of gunpowder on his right hand. It's possible he shot himself."

"My gut says murder staged to look like a suicide," Marc said. "When will the ME make a final determination?"

"Couple of days. Plus we have several techs and officers going through Lee's ransacked apartment, looking for any possible evidence linking him to the bank jobs."

"Good, I hope they find something. Did you verify the tattoo?"

"Yeah, and you're right, it looks similar to the one Jamison has," Miles agreed. "I'll keep you posted but wanted you to know we found him."

"I appreciate it."

"By the way, are you coming home for Sunday brunch?"

As much as he'd like to see his family, he couldn't risk exposing them, and Kari, to danger. "Not this week."

"I figured as much. I'll let Mom know."

"Thanks." Marc disconnected from the call, wondering about Lee's death. No way did he think the guy shot himself, but why kill him at all?

The only conclusion Marc could come to was

that there had to be another reason Kari's life was in danger. Not just because she identified the tattoo, but something more.

Was it possible she'd seen something else? Something that could help them identify who the third person was? If so, they needed to figure it out before it was too late.

THIRTEEN

When Kari heard the shrill ringing of Marc's phone, she slid off the bed and limped over to the connecting doorway so she could listen to his side of the conversation.

Goose bumps rippled down her arms when she heard that Tomas Lee was dead.

She closed her eyes for a moment and leaned against the door frame, wrestling with her chaotic emotions.

One of Jamison's suspected accomplices was dead, from either murder or suicide, leaving them with no other clues as to who else might be involved. A wave of helplessness washed over her. All of this death and destruction, for what? If the authorities were able to prove Tomas Lee was murdered, then she couldn't argue against the heightened threat of danger. His homicide only proved it was necessary for her to enter a witness-protection program.

She didn't want to go to a strange town, in

a different area of the country. Didn't want to leave her friends and her coworkers behind.

Especially Marc.

There was no logic to that thought, since it wasn't at all likely that she'd see Marc after the trial even if she wasn't forced to go into witness protection. She knew better than to read anything into their kiss. Hadn't she learned that lesson the hard way? Vince had professed to love her, but all along he'd intended only to take advantage of her.

Marc wasn't the kind of man who would take advantage of anyone, but he'd lost his wife and chosen to live in a world without color. Ridiculous to think their lives could ever mesh. Not to mention the small fact that he hadn't indicated he'd be interested in seeing her again, once this nightmare had ended.

Yet he was the one she'd miss the most. There were friends that she'd had much longer, but she suspected that they'd go on with their busy lives without missing her too much. She'd known Marc only a short time, but they'd grown close over the past few days. And no matter how much she tried, she couldn't forget the warmth of his embrace.

The heat of his kiss.

"Kari? Are you all right?"

The deep concern in Marc's voice forced her

eyes open. She tried, but failed, to manage a smile. "Not really. I feel terrible. I can't believe Tomas is dead."

"I know." Marc came closer and once again drew her into a tender embrace.

This time, she buried her face against his shoulder, absorbing his strength. He held her gently, but firmly, stroking a soothing hand down her back.

Despite the way she'd just tried to talk herself out of thinking about Marc as a man she could fall in love with, she snuggled close. Being held in his big, strong arms made her realize how much she longed for him to kiss her again.

Kari gathered the courage to tilt her head back to look up at him. His gaze locked on hers, and she imagined she could see the same desire she felt reflected in the green depths.

He hesitated and then slowly lowered his mouth to hers. His lips felt familiar now and she reveled in his kiss, sliding her hands up around his neck to hold on when her knees went weak. His sandalwood scent surrounded her and she knew she'd always remember him by it.

Long after he was gone, she's always remember this.

The kiss was far too brief. Marc lifted his head and rested his forehead against hers.

"Kari," he whispered roughly. "You're messing with my mind."

She couldn't help but smile. "Right back at you." Deep down inside, she was glad to know that he was struggling with their attraction as much as she was.

"What we're feeling right now isn't real," he went on, ruining the moment.

It was for her, but what could she say? He obviously didn't feel the same way.

He loosened his grip and then stepped away, putting distance between them. She let him go, and leaned against the door frame until her legs stopped feeling like limp noodles.

"I'd like to talk to you about the day of the bank robbery," he said.

Kari frowned at the abrupt change in subject and then made her way over to the small table. She dropped gratefully into the seat and gathered her scattered thoughts. If he wanted to ignore their kiss, then she would, too.

"What about it?" she asked, her tone sharper than she intended. "I went through every second of that day countless times, months ago. With both you and Detective Barclay."

"I know," he agreed, raking a hand through his dark hair. "But I keep wondering if we missed something."

"Like what?" She couldn't imagine they'd

missed anything about that day, especially since she'd been there as they went through the digital-camera images frame by frame.

"Lee's death makes me wonder if there isn't another reason they want you dead. More than just the fact that you were able to draw the likeness of Jamison's tattoo."

Dumbfounded, she stared at him. "I don't know what else they could possibly want from me," she said. "Watching the video stream of the bank that day didn't reveal anyone out of the ordinary. Just Jamison and a car that was waiting outside, the one they used to drive away." She wondered now if Tomas Lee had been the one driving the getaway car.

And why he had to die because of it.

"Okay, then think back to the time before the bank robbery," he prompted. "Is it possible you saw someone hanging around? Anything out of the ordinary?"

Kari slowly shook her head. "Not that I can recall," she admitted. "I was pretty upset because Vince had disappeared with all my money the previous week. All I remember is how angry and frustrated I was." The days before the robbery were nothing more than a blur. Marc was off base if he thought she'd remember anything of significance during that time frame.

It was amazing that she'd been alert enough to draw the tattoo she'd glimpsed on Jamison's chest.

"Okay, anything unusual that happened afterward? Maybe someone hanging around the bank, or outside your house?"

Kari closed her eyes and did her best to think back to those harried days after the bank robbery. She'd been interviewed by so many people, forced to repeat her story time and time again before the authorities were satisfied. She'd also been told to stay home from work on a paid leave for the rest of the week. Thankfully, her name hadn't been given to the media so she hadn't been forced to deal with reporters.

At least until two weeks before she was scheduled to testify, when suddenly her name had appeared in the newspaper as the key witness at Jamison's trial.

"I can't think of anything," she said finally, looking up at him with despair. "I went for long walks in the park, passed a few people here and there, but nothing that stands out in my mind."

"It's all right, I understand." He hesitated, then pressed for more. "Can you remember any details about the people you saw in the park?"

"What kind of details?" She couldn't hide her frustration. "They were just ordinary people. Mostly mothers pushing strollers or surrounded by little kids. I remember thinking that one day I'd be able to take my baby there, too."

"So no one that struck you as out of place?"

"Not really. There were some older couples I'd see, obviously retired. I did see one guy who wore a suit, which was a little odd since it was hot out that day, but he didn't seem to be paying any attention to me."

Marc's gaze sharpened. "What did the guy in the suit look like?"

Kari spread her hands helplessly. "Like a guy! In his thirties or forties, brown hair. I can't tell you anything more than that. Besides, I only saw him once, in the middle of the week. I doubt he's involved."

"Could you draw him?"

"No, I can't. Sorry, but I don't remember really looking at his face. I just remember the fleeting thought that he must be hot in his suit and tie. He was probably just taking a quick lunch break or something. He certainly didn't strike me as nervous or anything like that."

Marc let out a heavy sigh. "You're right, I'm grasping at straws. It's just frustrating to think that you might be a target simply because the guy behind the robberies thinks you know something that you don't."

"Tell me about it," she muttered harshly. She wished she could remember something important because then they could put this guy behind bars.

With the elimination of that threat, she for sure wouldn't have to go into witness protection.

Leaving her entire life behind.

The next day dragged slowly as Marc stared at his computer screen, trying to think of another angle to pursue to investigate the leak within the task force. Tomas Lee, their only lead, was dead.

Maybe he should go back to the tattoo shop to see if Mikio had more information related to the second man. He'd have to risk facing the man and his razor-sharp sword, and doubted that pulling his gun would encourage Mikio to cooperate. Besides, if the tattoo artist only dealt with cash, then there wouldn't be anything to link to the identity of the second man.

Which left him with nothing.

Except, of course, the need to keep Kari safe for the next two days, until she was needed to testify.

"Why don't you relax a bit?" he suggested. "Maybe watch a movie or something?"

She wrinkled her nose. "There hasn't been much to see. I don't particularly like scary or violent movies."

"Come on, there has to be a Christmas movie

in there somewhere," Marc urged, drawing her up to her feet.

"I'd love to see *It's a Wonderful Life*," she said in a wistful tone.

Marc was ashamed to admit that he'd never watched the film. He wasn't sure how he'd missed it, when everyone else on the planet had seen it, but he had. Obviously, Jess was right about how he'd worked too much.

"Can't hurt to check," he said as they walked into her room.

"I like the original version the best," she said, stretching out on the bed and once again elevating her ankle. "No one plays George Bailey like Jimmy Stewart."

Marc picked up the remote and flipped through the channels. "Jimmy Stewart? Just how old is this movie?"

"Old. Really old."

"Here it is, in the queue for movies on demand." Marc pushed the button to start the show.

"Isn't there an added charge for that?" she protested.

"I'll submit it to my expense account."

That made her laugh, and once the movie began, he soon found himself engrossed in the story. He pulled up a chair to sit beside her.

The movie was sad in parts, but thankfully had a happy ending with the theme that family was important. Marc had always known that, and the Callahan clan was a close-knit bunch. But he hadn't always practiced that with Jessica.

Until it was too late.

Now he realized that the secrets he'd kept relating to Jessica's affair and the resulting pregnancy had driven a bit of a wedge between him and the rest of his family.

His fault, not theirs. His mom, Nan and siblings had given him room to grieve his wife's tragic death. It had been easier to let them believe that than to tell them the truth.

He couldn't bear the thought of seeing pity reflected in their eyes.

"That was wonderful, thanks," Kari said on a sigh, wiping away a stray tear.

"You don't have to thank me. It's the least I can do." Marc tried to soften the edge that had crept into his tone. "We're going to be stuck here for the next two nights, so go ahead and watch whatever holiday movies you like."

"To be honest with you, what I'd really like is to go to church," Kari said, a hesitant expression in her eyes, as if she expected him to deny her simple request.

He shouldn't have been surprised by her desire to attend church services, after all, the next day was Sunday, but he was. His first instinct was to suggest the same church the Callahans always attended, but of course, that wouldn't be smart. The last thing he wanted to do was to expose his family to danger; his brothers had gone out on a limb to help him enough already.

"Which church would you like to attend?" he asked quietly.

"The one I've been going to since Vince left me. It's not too far from my house." Her large brown eyes pleaded with him. "The people there are so nice, even knowing my situation. They've never once made me feel uncomfortable."

He didn't like the thought of anyone treating her badly because of her situation, yet at the same time, he couldn't agree to her plan. "I'm sorry, Kari. It's not a good idea for us to attend a church you've been to before, and one located so close to your house. We can't rule out the possibility that this guy is watching your place."

Her face fell, but she nodded. "Okay, I can understand that, but can we find one similar to the one I normally attend?"

"Yeah, that should be okay. I'll get my computer—you can do a search, see what you find."

Kari's gaze was intense as she surfed the internet. It seemed to take a long time, almost a half hour, before she turned the screen to face him. "How about here?"

The church was simple yet beautiful, with a tall brown steeple topped with a cross. He leaned closer, checking out the address. It happened to be located in the opposite side of town from her home and far enough from his family's church that he had no concerns about being seen.

"Looks great to me."

"Thanks, Marc," she said with a misty smile. Then she wiped at her face. "I don't know what's wrong with me. I've been so emotional lately."

"It's okay. I don't mind." He lightly stroked her cheek, then pulled back, before he did anything stupid. He jotted own the address of the church on a slip of hotel stationary, then stuffed it into his pocket. "Are you hungry? We ate a late dinner, but I can still go out and get something else for you. Or we can eat what's left of the pizza."

She wrinkled her nose and shook her head. "No, thanks. I'm fine. I'll try to get some sleep."

Oddly disappointed that they wouldn't be spending more time together that evening, Marc nodded and returned to his room, carrying his computer.

The investigation was stalled, and at this point there wasn't anything more he could do to find the man who'd killed Tomas. He needed to focus his energy on finding a safe way to get Kari inside the courtroom to testify.

He couldn't bear the thought of anything happening to her. He refused to lose another witness the way he'd lost Joey Simmons three years ago, during the five-mile drive to the courthouse in his own personal vehicle.

No, this time, he'd have a better plan. For one thing, he'd be driving Kari to the courthouse in the truck, which no one would recognize. Or maybe he'd even ask one of his brothers to swap cars with him, so that they'd be in a completely different vehicle.

And he'd use the underground parking garage, taking Kari past the concrete posts then up through the back stairwell. He could picture the route in his mind, and knew he'd need plenty of backup.

He reached for his phone and called Miles again.

"Something wrong?" Miles asked abruptly, giving Marc the impression he'd interrupted him in the middle of something important.

"No, sorry, nothing like that. But I do need some help on Monday morning to get Kari safely into the courthouse." Marc knew he probably should have begun planning the route sooner. "I hate to ask, but do you think it's possible you can get off work that day? I'd like some backup, both before and after she's finished testifying."

"I can call in a few favors," his brother said with a sigh. "What about Mitch or Mike? Did you ask them to help out, too?"

"I left them both messages earlier, but they didn't call me back." He knew his brothers were busy with their respective careers, but he'd hoped they'd get in touch before now. "I can try them again."

"No, don't worry about it. I'll fill them in on what you need," Miles said. "Anything else?"

"That's all for now, but I'll need to talk to all three of you later tomorrow, just for an hour or so, to go through the plan."

"We'll swing by after brunch," Miles promised.

"Thanks." Marc was touched by his brother's willingness to drop everything to help him. Of course he'd do the same for them, but he couldn't help thinking about the fact that Kari didn't have anyone willing to step out on a limb for her. No parents, no siblings.

Just him. The responsibility of keeping her safe rested solely on his shoulders. And he was determined to do his best for Kari.

Or die trying.

FOURTEEN

Despite her bone-weary exhaustion, Kari didn't sleep well. By the time light peeked in around the heavy curtains over the window, she gave up and crawled out of bed.

Testing her ankle, she was surprised and pleased that she was able to bear weight with hardly any pain. The swelling had also gone down dramatically, but she still walked with care as she made her way into the bathroom.

Thirty minutes later, she emerged refreshed and hungry. She crossed over to the connecting door and pressed her ear to the small opening, listening for any sound that indicated Marc might be awake.

Silence.

Glancing at her watch, she realized it was barely six thirty. Unfortunately, she had no idea how long Marc had worked into the night.

Deciding to let him sleep, she went back over to the desk to page through the hotel directory for local restaurants. When she discovered the hotel offered a free continental breakfast, she blew out a sigh of relief. Now she wouldn't have to go outside by herself. She could simply go to the lobby. At almost nineteen weeks along, her morning sickness had passed, but a hint of nausea remained in the early hours of the day, especially when her stomach was empty. It was as if her body was warning her to hurry up and feed the baby.

With a wry smile, she quickly scribbled a note for Marc, in case he woke up while she was gone. She set it on her pillow, then scooped up the room key along with her prenatal vitamins and crossed over to the door.

When she stepped into the hallway, a cold breeze caught her off guard, and she realized there must be an outside door open somewhere close by. She assumed someone had propped it open to make it easier to move luggage either in or out. She shivered and crossed her arms over her chest as she walked down the hall toward the lobby.

The room was cheery and smelled good; the breakfast offerings lining the far wall were better than she'd expected. Her stomach rumbled loudly as she eagerly helped herself to fluffy scrambled eggs, toast and a yogurt.

Several tables were set up and she took a seat,

gave a quick silent prayer of thanks, and took a bite of the eggs. Not great, but certainly edible. When she'd finished eating, she took her giant vitamin with a glass of milk and sat back in her seat, feeling much better. She cleaned up her breakfast dishes, then debated whether she should bother with a cup of decaf coffee.

Someone came into the lobby bringing a wave of cold air, so she went ahead and filled a coffee mug for warmth as much as anything. She sat back down, loath to return to the impersonal hotel room.

There was a television mounted in the corner of the room where most of the patrons could see it. The local news was on and she nearly dropped her coffee when Jamison's mug shot flashed on the screen.

Maybe she should have expected the trial to be one of the top news stories. After all, by tomorrow morning, the federal courthouse would be jammed with media as she took the witness stand.

The sick feeling in her stomach returned and she set down her mug then pushed it away. What if her picture was plastered on the screen, too? Everyone in the hotel would stare at her, knowing that she was about to testify against Jamison.

She needed to get out of here. Now!

Keeping her head down, she rose to her feet.

As she turned toward the doorway leading out to the hallway, she saw the tall, muscular frame of Marc striding rapidly toward her.

"There you are! I've been worried sick," he said in an accusatory tone.

"I left a note." She noticed his gaze had zeroed in on the television screen behind her. The scowl etched in his ruggedly handsome features deepened as he realized Jamison was the leading news story. "Come on, we need to go back," she said in a low tone.

He gave a terse nod, stepping aside so she could precede him. She walked quickly, relieved her ankle was up to the pace, as they returned to their adjoining rooms.

Marc muttered something under his breath that sounded like *blood-thirsty reporters*. Kari couldn't help but agree. Obviously, they were willing to do anything, even if that meant putting her life in danger, for the sake of a good story that would increase ratings.

"Pack your things," Marc said curtly. "We need to check out of here."

"Maybe you should grab something to eat first," Kari said, gathering the few items she possessed. "It's free."

"No need. I'll eat the leftover pizza."

She nodded, then realized the note she'd left on the pillow was lying on the floor. The breeze must have sent it fluttering away. She awkwardly bent down to pick it up, her stomach seeming to have gotten more rounded in the past few days. "Here's my note. I'm sorry you were worried."

Marc grimaced and took the slip of paper from her fingers. "I'm sorry I yelled," he said in a low, husky tone. "I panicked when I thought I'd lost you."

Their gazes clashed and held for endless seconds and she could easily see the worry and apprehension reflected in the green depths. Her breath strangled in her throat at his obvious concern for her safety.

Because she was his witness? Or because of the bond that had grown between them?

She leaned forward, as if to move into his arms, but he broke the connection between them by turning abruptly away. "I'll grab my computer," he mumbled over his shoulder.

He disappeared from sight, leaving her alone.

Her feet rooted to the floor, Kari wrestled with her hormonal emotions. Ridiculous to be upset that he hadn't caught her into his arms. Hadn't kissed her.

Wasn't it enough that he was protecting her? Of course it was.

Shaking off the odd depression, she forced herself to do one last sweep of the small hotel room, making sure she had everything she needed. When her small bag was full, she crossed over to Marc's room.

The pizza box was lying open on the table with nothing but crumbs left behind, evidence that he'd already finished the leftovers. The duffel bag was sitting on the top of his bed, and he reached out a hand for her things, tucking them inside.

"Ready?" he asked, tossing the strap of the duffel over his shoulder.

Unable to trust her voice, she silently nodded. Within five minutes, they were back outside and seated in the large truck. This time, she'd gotten into the seat under her own volition, thanks to her healing ankle.

Silence stretched uncomfortably between them as Marc drove away, leaving the hotel behind them. Kari stared out the passenger-side window, absorbing the Christmas spirit decorating the houses they drove past. The city streets had little to no traffic this early on a Sunday.

Church services weren't for another hour and a half, and she hoped Marc hadn't changed his mind about attending.

Fifteen minutes later, he slowed the truck down as he approached a church. She frowned, thinking it didn't look like the one she'd found online, but she wasn't about to argue, either.

"That's the church my family attends," he

said, breaking the strained silence. "We've been going there since I was a young boy."

"It looks beautiful," she said, taking in the intricate stained glass windows and the Christmas lights hanging from the trees. "I wish you could join your family."

He nodded then shrugged. "Next time."

She wondered if he'd married his wife there, and if returning every week was a painful reminder. He hadn't mentioned much about his wife, not even how she'd died.

The truck picked up speed, and the church disappeared behind them. Twenty minutes later, he pulled up to the church she recognized from her internet search.

"It's early, but I thought maybe we could go inside anyway for a while," he said.

"I'd like that." Kari pushed open her door, then frowned when she saw how high up off the ground she was. She didn't want to jump, fearing she'd hurt her ankle again.

"I've got you," Marc said, placing his hands beneath her armpits. She clung to his biceps as he lowered her gently on the ground.

"Thank you," she murmured, her pulse skipping erratically in her chest.

Marc surprised her by keeping a steady hand around her waist as they approached the front door. He held it open for her, and the moment she entered the church a sense of calm and joy surged through her.

She stood for a moment, soaking in the beauty of the simple altar and crucifix at the front of the church and absorbing the amazing sensation of being in God's house. Placing a protective hand over her rounded belly, Kari knew this was exactly what she needed.

Peace, hope and love.

An odd sense of welcoming embraced Marc as he entered the church a few steps behind Kari. He didn't understand why, since he'd never been inside this particular church before. At first he thought maybe his feelings were tied to Kari, but then he wondered if this was God's way of receiving him back into his faith.

He followed Kari as she stepped forward and slid into one of the long pews. Taking a seat beside her, he was struck by the fact that it felt right to be with Kari like this.

Was this what had been missing in his marriage? When he thought of his marriage to Jessica compared to the union of his parents, he knew now that something had been missing. Even after thirty years of marriage, his parents held a united front, one of deep abiding love and faith.

Not that he was foolish enough to think their

marriage had been perfect, because he knew it wasn't. Even after they were all grown and becoming established in their various careers, there had been some troubled times between his mom and dad, especially when it came to Michael.

Max Callahan had made it clear Michael's decision to become a private investigator wasn't good enough. Didn't follow in the Callahan legacy of serving their community. Michael acted as if he didn't care, refusing to reconsider attending the police academy the way their father had pressured him to, but Marc knew better.

And so did their mother, Maggie. She'd stood by Mike's choice regardless of the fact that it was in direct opposition of her husband's. Marc admired their mother for her unwavering and unconditional love for their children.

Glancing at Kari, he was struck by the knowledge that she would be the same way, loving her baby no matter the sins of the father. Could he have done that with Jessica? Forgiven her sins enough to love the child despite the lack of a blood bond between them?

Shame had him hanging his head as he acknowledged how difficult that would have been. Maybe not impossible, but still not easy.

A man dressed in dark clothes came into the church from behind the altar. He appeared surprised to see them, but didn't interrupt, instead readying the church for the upcoming service. Fifteen minutes later, parishioners began to filter in.

A small choir began to sing, and Marc was startled by his desire to join in. Strange how he'd forgotten how much he enjoyed singing hymns, something he hadn't been interested in since Jessica's death.

The pastor began his sermon by speaking of the first Sunday of Advent.

"Repent, my fellow parishioners, repent! Turn away from sin and darkness, instead turning to the light of God."

Marc wondered if the pastor could see right through to his heart, to the fact that he had turned away from lightness and God since Jessica had died and he'd found out the truth about her pregnancy. When he should have done the exact opposite.

As the pastor continued, Marc absorbed every word, every phrase, every prayer.

"Remember that God has accepted each of us just the way we are. We were received when we were less than worthy and now must do the same for those around us. My request of you is to do the same. 'Welcome one another, therefore, just as Christ has welcomed you, for the glory of God,' Romans 15:7."

For a moment Marc's heart stuttered before it

resumed its rhythmic beat. Long after the service ended, the pastor's words echoed over and over in his mind.

Accept and forgive.

When the final hymn was sung, Marc stepped into the aisle and then stood to the side, waiting for Kari to precede him. Once again, he followed her back outside to the small parking lot.

An older woman in front of Kari slipped on a patch of ice. She might have fallen if not for Kari's quick thinking. She grabbed the woman's arm, steadying her.

"Oh, thank you, dearie."

Marc came up on the woman's other side. "Here, hang on to me. Which car is yours?"

"Thank you, young man. That's my husband now in the white Dodge. He told me to wait, but standing around doing nothing isn't easy for me."

Marc hid a smile. "Be careful now," he cautioned as she stepped up to the car. He reached out and opened the door for her.

"Thank you, again. You two make such a cute couple. Merry Christmas!"

"Merry Christmas," he said in unison with Kari, making the woman laugh.

After the woman's husband drove away, he took Kari's arm as they made their way over to the spot where he'd parked the truck. He didn't want Kari falling, the way the churchgoer almost had.

"You were pretty quiet in church. Are you all right?" she asked, her eyes filled with concern.

"I'm fine," he assured her. "That was nice."

A smile bloomed on her face, and her beauty stole his breath. "I'm so glad," she said. "I was afraid you were comparing today's service in an unfavorable light to what you normally experience at your parents' church."

"Never," he said, his voice husky with emotion. He opened her door and assisted her into the truck before going around to the driver's side to climb in beside her. He turned on the engine, giving it several minutes to warm up. "I need to thank you for picking out this church," he said. "I have to be honest—I needed to hear that message."

"Really? I'm glad to hear that, but I'm a little confused as to why the sermon resonated so much with you."

He paused, then decided it was time she knew the truth. "I told you I lost my wife two years ago, but I didn't tell you everything."

Kari reached over to take his hand in hers. "Go on," she encouraged.

"Our marriage was great the first year, but then things began to change. Jessica wanted to attend parties and have fun, and she grew to re-sent the time I spent working. I was just starting my career and wanted to make a good impression with the Special Agent in Charge."

"That's understandable," she murmured.

"Jess didn't agree. And it wasn't just the hours I worked. I preferred spending time at home, being together with just the two of us, but Jess thought that was boring and insisted we go out. I encouraged her to go on her own, so she did."

"Uh-oh," she muttered.

"Yeah, that wasn't the smartest move I ever made," he agreed in a wry tone. "I thought some sort of compromise would make her happy, but it turned out the exact opposite. She began flaunting the fact that other men were interested in her, and that she could have her pick of the bunch."

Kari's fingers tightened around his and for a long moment he stared at their clasped hands, amazed at how easy it was to talk to her.

"Well, you can guess what happened then," he said gruffly. "I asked her to consider counseling, but she refused, telling me that I was the problem."

"That's not right," Kari said sharply. "It wasn't as if she didn't have faults. Besides, couples therapy is all about opening the lines of communication. Difficult to do, if she's not even around to talk to."

Her staunch support humbled him, especially

because he knew he didn't deserve it. Although Kari was right in that Jessica had her share of problems, too. "Thank you, but I know I worked too much. I came home late one night to find several squad cars outside our house. In my heart I knew something was terribly wrong, but I wasn't prepared to hear that Jessica had crashed her car into a tree." He swallowed a lump in his throat. "They told me alcohol played a role in her death, and I always wondered if she'd finally decided to leave me that night."

"Oh, Marc, I'm so sorry," Kari whispered.

He nodded, knowing he had to finish it. "The worst part was finding out later that she was pregnant. Three months along."

She drew in a harsh breath, her free hand coming up to rest on her stomach. "That's terrible."

"Yeah. But the fact is, I suspected the child wasn't mine. I requested DNA evidence, which proved it." He risked glancing over at her, gauging her reaction. "I shouldn't have been surprised she cheated on me. After all, I was the one who told her to go ahead and attend the various parties alone. But it was still a shock."

"I—I don't know what to say."

"You don't have to say anything. The sermon today helped me to understand that accepting ourselves for the way we are is the first step toward forgiveness."

She nodded, her hand clinging to his. "I'm glad you heard that message, but I hope you realize that it's not just about forgiving Jessica. It's about forgiving yourself, too."

Her words hit him like a brick to his chest. Why hadn't he realized it before? All this time he'd been harboring a deep resentment toward Jessica for sleeping with other men and getting pregnant, but now he realized that he was mostly angry with himself.

"You're right, Kari. I don't know exactly how to forgive myself for the role I played in my wife's death, but I'll try."

"Just remember, her sins aren't your fault. You can forgive yourself for working too much, putting your career ahead of your marriage, but you can't take all the blame. Two people working together and loving one another is the only way to make a marriage work."

He knew she was right. After all, wasn't that the epitome of how his parents had lived?

"Thanks, Kari." He reluctantly released her hand to put the truck into gear. "We'd better find another place to stay."

She nodded and he backed out of the parking space and then drove back out onto the street. As he approached the next intersection, he noticed a squad car coming up behind him.

His gut knotted with tension. After a long

minute, the cop suddenly put on his lights and hit the siren.

They were being pulled over? Why? Marc waited for the light to turn green, inwardly debating whether he should try to lose the cop. When the signal changed, he moved forward enough to clear the intersection then pulled over to the right-hand side of the road.

"What's going on?" Kari asked.

"I don't know. I don't think I broke any traffic laws." Marc lowered his window, then placed his hands in plain sight on the top of the steering wheel. When the officer approached, Marc glanced up at him. "Good morning, officer. What seems to be the problem?"

"Driver's license and registration," the officer barked.

Marc carefully reached into his hip pocket to remove his wallet. His badge was in his coat pocket, but he wasn't sure he wanted to bring out the FBI card just yet.

Kari rummaged in the glove box, finding the registration paperwork. Marc's heart sank when he realized that Garrett's name was listed, instead of his.

"Please step out of the vehicle," the officer ordered.

"Will you tell me what this is about?" Marc asked, trying to hide his frustration.

"It's about the fact that you're driving a stolen truck. Now get out and put your hands up."

Stolen? Impossible for Garrett to have reported it stolen from Afghanistan.

The driver of the black SUV that had tailed him outside his condo must have run the plates, putting an APB out for his arrest.

Marc complied with the officer's directive, trying to figure out a way to avoid being tossed in jail, leaving Kari vulnerable and alone.

FIFTEEN

Kari's pulse raced with fear and trepidation as she watched Marc slide out from behind the wheel, holding his hands up in the air the way the cop had told him to.

"I'm a federal agent," he said in an authoritative tone.

"I don't care who you are. This is a stolen vehicle," the cop snapped. "Now keep your hands where I can see them."

She dug in her pocket for her phone, quickly dialing Miles's number. It rang twice before he answered. "Yeah? What's up?"

"Miles, a cop pulled us over and I think he's going to arrest Marc."

"What? Why?"

"He claims Mitch's friend's truck has been stolen."

"Can you see his badge?" Miles asked. "What's the number?"

"His last name is Plato, his badge number

is 478. We're on the corner of Howell and Seventy-Sixth Street."

"I know Greg Plato. I want to talk to him."

Kari swallowed hard and leaned over the center console. "Officer Plato? I have Miles Callahan on the phone. He'd like to talk to you."

"Callahan?" Officer Plato looked surprised, then frowned, looking down at Marc's wallet that he still held in his hand. "You're Marcus Callahan?"

"Yes. And the woman with me is a key witness against a man suspected of serial bank robberies," Marc said, still holding his hands up, palms facing outward. "This truck isn't stolen, either. Garrett Rolland is in the Marines, doing time in Afghanistan. He also happens to be a friend of Mitch's."

"Please talk to Miles?" Kari pleaded. "We're in danger sitting here like this."

Officer Plato muttered a curse under his breath but reached for her phone. "Callahan? What's going on?"

She tried to catch Marc's gaze, but he was looking around the area, alert to the possibility of a threat. Would the man responsible for the leak inside the task force wait for Marc to be brought down for questioning? Or was he right now hiding somewhere nearby with a gun trained on her?

Shivering in the passenger-side seat, Kari waited for Officer Plato to come to his senses. His scowl deepened as he listened to whatever Miles was telling him.

"Okay, okay. Thanks." The officer handed the phone back to her through the open window. "I trust your brother, so I'm letting you go. But you need to do something about the license plate, or you'll just get pulled over by some other cop."

"Understood, thank you," Marc said, holding out a hand for his wallet. "I appreciate your assistance."

"Yeah, I'll call it in as a false alarm, the way Miles suggested," Officer Plato said on a sigh. "Get rid of those plates ASAP, understand?"

"Do you have any tools with you?" Marc asked. "I'll take them off right now."

The officer hesitated, as if he didn't want to get too involved, then he shrugged. "Sure, just a sec."

Marc flashed her a reassuring smile, then followed the officer back to his squad. Ten minutes later, they were back on the road, sans license plate.

"I'm not sure how this helps. We can still get pulled over for not having it, right?" Kari said, clenching her fingers together nervously.

"True. We'll find a motel and then see if Miles can bring us a replacement."

She nodded and tried to relax. What would she do without the Callahans? She and Marc would never have gotten this far without the help of his family.

As he drove, she kept her eyes glued to the side-view mirror, half expecting to see a cop car coming up behind them at any moment. When her phone rang a few minutes later, she startled so badly she dropped it.

To pick it up, she had to bend sideways, making her realize all over again that her belly was getting bigger. Did it always happen this way, that one minute your stomach didn't seem too big, the next it popped out like a basketball?

"Hello?" she asked breathlessly.

"It's Miles. Where are you?"

"Officer Plato let us go, and we took the license plates off, too. We're looking for a new hotel."

"Put the phone on speaker so I can talk to Marc."

Kari complied, holding the phone between them.

"Thanks, Miles, I'm glad you happened to know that guy," Marc said in a grim tone.

"Yeah, well, it's not good that Garrett's truck is listed as stolen. How did they get the plate numbers, anyway?"

Marc explained how he'd gone to his condo

and was briefly followed by a black SUV with tinted windows, much like the one that had followed them earlier. "I can only assume that the driver ran the plates, and realized that Garrett had ties to Mitch, and therefore to me. Then he must have decided to report the truck as stolen as a way to track me down."

Miles let out a low whistle. "I don't like it, bro. Not one bit."

"Me neither," Marc agreed. "I'm hoping you can bring me replacement license plates when you come by later."

"Sure, no problem." Miles's tone held a distinct sarcasm. "We have dozens of license plates just lying around waiting to be used."

"Do you know a good place for us to stay?" Kari asked.

"There's a place way out in the country, off Highway 177, called the Shamrock Inn."

"I know where it is," Marc agreed. "Good idea. We'll get settled there. Give us a call when you're ready to leave Mom's."

"She's not happy you skipped out on brunch," Miles said. "But don't worry, we downplayed the danger. Mitch is coming with me, Matthew is still in K9 training and Michael is hot on some other case."

"Thanks. See you soon."

Kari disconnected from the call, glad that two

of Marc's brothers would be there to help. Marc needed backup and she was useless when it came to anything related to law enforcement.

"The Shamrock Inn is a good twenty-minute ride from here," Marc told her. "Why don't you try to get some sleep?"

She wrinkled her nose at him. "As if I can sleep after being stopped by the police like that," she scoffed. "Not likely."

"That was a close call," Marc muttered. "I should have thought of swapping the license plates sooner."

Too close, she silently agreed. If she hadn't called Miles, she was certain that Officer Plato would have arrested Marc despite his being with the FBI.

"We didn't know for certain the SUV outside your condo belonged to the gunmen," she reminded him. "Especially when they backed off, leaving us alone."

"Pretending to leave us alone," Marc said harshly. "I should have anticipated they'd run the plates and figure out that Garrett was Mitch's friend."

"We're fine now," she soothed, wishing he wouldn't be so hard on himself. Was this the intensity that drove him to work long hours, leaving his wife to find her fun elsewhere? Not that she believed his wife's actions were at all justified.

Marc's jaw tightened but he didn't say anything further.

Kari couldn't help thinking back to his earlier confession, about his wife's affair and the baby she'd carried that he hadn't fathered. Her heart went out to him for the anguish he'd suffered.

She truly wanted him to forgive Jessica, and more so to forgive himself. But hearing his story had given her the impression that even if she'd lived, he wouldn't have been able to accept the baby as his.

A fluttering in her abdomen distracted her and she slipped her hand beneath her coat to press against the tiny movements. They seemed stronger now, as if her baby was gaining weight day by day.

Rubbing her hand over her stomach, she told herself that it was a good thing she knew the truth about Marc's wife. No wonder he lived in such austere surroundings. And if he couldn't accept his wife's pregnancy, demanding a DNA test, she doubted he'd be willing to take on another baby that wasn't his.

Had she really thought there was a chance he would? That his kisses had meant something more than offering comfort during a time of stress? Okay, maybe there was a bit of a connection between them, but she couldn't afford to call it anything other than friendship.

She should be honored to have Marc as a friend. So why did she yearn for something more?

Her heart wrenched in her chest, but she ignored it. Hadn't she decided that she was better off raising her baby alone? Her mother had done a great job with raising her; she needed to do the same for this child.

She was so lost in her thoughts, she didn't realize that Marc had pulled into the parking lot of the less than prestigious Shamrock Inn.

From what she could tell, there were barely ten rooms total and the outside of the building looked as if it could use several coats of new paint. The *m* in the Shamrock was burned out, but the vacancy sign was lit up in the lobby window.

"Stay here. I'll be back shortly," Marc said.

She nodded, not willing to risk anyone recognizing her, even here, way out of the city. She could only imagine how much press the story was getting and many people were news junkies.

It seemed like a long time before Marc returned to the truck. He slid into the seat and made a U-turn, driving around to the back of the building.

"Problems?" she asked.

"No, we have our two connecting rooms," he said, releasing a ragged breath. "But it took me a while to convince the clerk to allow us to park in back. Apparently, business is slow and she wanted the truck parked out front to prove they have guests."

She lifted a brow. "You'd think they'd be busy in the two weeks before Christmas."

He shrugged and set the computer on the desk and the duffel on the bed. He removed the plastic bag she'd used for her things and handed it to her. "Is there anything else you need?"

"No, thanks." Even if she did want something she wouldn't tell him. There was no sense in Marc driving around in the truck with no license plates.

She crossed the threshold between their rooms, suppressing a sigh. The place smelled musty, as if the rooms hadn't been used recently. At least they'd only be here one night.

Her stomach tightened at the thought of testifying in court first thing in the morning. For so long now, they'd been focused on staying one step ahead of the gunmen.

The prosecutor had gone over her testimony several times with her, before the night she'd been forced to go on the run. She knew Jamison's defense attorney, a high-powered lawyer out of Chicago, would go after her character and challenge her memory of that day.

Twenty-four hours, she reminded herself.

Twenty-four hours and she'd be finished with her testimony.

And then she'd be forced to go into witness protection, leaving behind her life as she knew it.

Marc contacted his brothers, reminding them to bring the replacement license plates. At least they'd only need them for a short time. Once Kari testified, he'd turn her over to witness protection and they'd do their job of creating a new identity for her.

He didn't like that plan, but it was better than having her be in danger from whoever was trying to silence her.

Logically, she shouldn't be in danger once she'd testified, but nothing about this situation made sense. Why come after Kari, when it would be easier to take out Jamison?

No, he kept coming back to the fact that Kari must have seen something that pointed to the identity of the leak inside the task force.

A sharp rapping on his door interrupted his thoughts. He crossed over and put his eye to the peephole to make sure his brothers were the ones out there.

"Thanks for coming," Marc said, opening the door for Miles and Mitch to enter.

"No biggie," Mitch said with a shrug. "You'd do the same for us."

He would, and was thankful for the Callahan legacy of family that their parents had instilled within them. Mitch held the license plates in his hand. "Where's the truck? I'll swap these out before we get to work."

"In the back," Marc told him.

"Where's our pretty witness?" Miles asked with a broad smile.

"Your charm is wasted on me, Miles Callahan," Kari said from the doorway. "But I'll give you brownie points for trying."

His brother didn't seem fazed by her comments. "Actually, I have good news for you. The Chicago Police have Vince Ackerman, aka Andrew Volkman, aka numerous other aliases in custody for theft. He's facing several counts, and more women are coming forward every day. He'll do hard time for what he's done."

Kari's smile faded and she once again put her hand on her abdomen. "I see. Thanks for letting me know."

Miles's eyes widened, and he turned to glance at Marc. "Is she…" His voice trailed off.

"Yes, I am almost nineteen weeks pregnant," Kari said drily. "Tried to tell you not to waste your charm on me."

"I'm just surprised, that's all," Miles said defensively. He turned toward Marc. "You're right. We need a foolproof plan to get her into the courthouse safely."

"Yeah," Marc agreed. "Let's get to work."

When Mitch returned a few minutes later, Marc outlined his plan. "I want to bring Kari in through the underground parking structure, limiting the ability for a sniper shot."

"Yeah, I agree," Miles said in a serious tone. "But we'll need to get in there super early, to make sure there isn't anyone hiding down there."

Marc nodded. "And I want Kari to wear body armor."

Miles frowned. "Not sure that will help protect her baby."

"Baby?" Mitch echoed in surprise.

"Yeah, she's pregnant. Which means we need to protect both of them."

Mitch whistled, then nodded. "Okay. What else?"

"I want you both to promise me something," Marc said, keeping his voice low so Kari wouldn't hear.

"What?" Miles asked.

"No matter what happens to me, I want you to promise you'll get Kari to safety. I want you to stay with her during her testimony and afterward, until she's taken into custody by the US Marshals."

His brothers exchanged a long look. "No way are we leaving you behind, bro," Miles said.

"Listen, Kari is the innocent victim here," Marc said in a harsh whisper. "She's pregnant and without her testimony Jamison will walk. So yeah, I absolutely expect you to protect her at all costs, understand? No matter what."

"Fine, we'll abide by your wishes," Mitch said in a grim tone. "But we need to make sure we're all wearing body armor."

Miles scowled but nodded reluctantly. "Okay, okay. Are you sure we don't have any clues as to who the leak is? If we could nail him, then Kari wouldn't be a target."

"There are three potential suspects," Marc admitted. "But absolutely no proof against any of them. Just financial troubles, that's all."

"Greed is often the primary motive for murder," Miles said.

"I know, but since Jamison isn't talking, we don't know which one of them is the leak," Marc admitted. "And honestly, the person on the task force easily could have mentioned something to a family member. The leak might not have been intentional."

"What does your gut say?" Mitch asked.

He hesitated. "Steve Young has just gotten divorced and David Hermes is a year behind on his child-support payments. Monique Barclay also has bad debt, but when I dug into her background it seems that most of her bad debt is related to loans she cosigned with her younger sister. Maybe it's sexist, but I can't see Monique getting involved in a series of bank robberies."

"It is sexist," Mitch spoke up. "But unfortunately, based on what you've told us, I'm inclined to agree with you."

"Steve Young and David Hermes, huh?" Miles said. "I can't say I've met either one of them."

"Me neither," Mitch acknowledged. "But we can probably find pictures of them online."

Miles went to work on the computer, while Mitch and Marc watched. It didn't take Miles long to pull up images of both men. Seeing Steve Young in his dress police uniform and David Hermes wearing a dark suit and tie, he doubted his wisdom in making these two his top suspects all over again.

They both had too much to lose by participating in bank robberies. Yet at the same time, Marc knew that desperate people often did desperate things.

"These guys look like your average cops to me," Mitch said in disgust. "Why would they risk smearing their reputations?"

"I don't know," Marc said.

"Let's see if we can dig into their backgrounds a bit more," Miles suggested.

"I'm game," Mitch agreed.

Marc sat back, letting Miles work on the computer. When it was clear that the search would take a while, he excused himself to go check on Kari.

Her room was quiet, so he stepped carefully across the threshold. He found her curled up on top of her bed, with the motel bible lying open next to her, sound asleep.

His fingers itched to push the dark strands of hair away from her face, but he forced himself to stay put. He didn't want to risk waking her, knowing she needed her rest.

Yet he couldn't seem to walk away. Instead he once again watched her sleep, trying not to think about the fact that by this time tomorrow, she'd be whisked off by the US Marshals under a completely different identity.

An identity that he'd never know, since the US Marshals prided themselves on their secrecy, claiming that their methods were what had kept all their witnesses safe over so many years.

Even an FBI agent wouldn't be allowed to know her new name. Marc felt his chest tighten, silently admitting just how much he was going to miss her. More than he thought possible.

Somehow, despite the way he'd hardened his heart after Jessica's affair and subsequent death, a petite pregnant woman had managed to wiggle her way through the crusty outer shell.

Making him feel emotions he thought were long dead and buried.

SIXTEEN

When Kari woke up, the room was still dark. She angled her head to check out the red numbers on the small alarm clock.

It took a few seconds for the time to register. Barely five o'clock in the morning. Remembering Marc's plan to get to the courthouse early, she dragged herself out of bed and made her way to the bathroom.

She emerged twenty minutes later, trying to push away the sick feeling of doom. Kari trusted Marc to keep her safe, but she also knew that once she'd testified, her life as she knew it would be over.

"Good morning," Marc said, hovering in the doorway between their rooms. "Did you sleep okay?"

She forced a smile. "Yes. One thing about being pregnant is that sleep comes much easier."

"I'm glad," Marc murmured, his gaze dropping down to her stomach, hidden by the bulky sweater she wore. "Mitch is bringing breakfast. We'll talk about the plan for getting you into the courthouse while we eat."

"All right." She tucked a strand of hair behind her ear and walked over to his room. "Did your brothers stay all night?"

"They did. They shared the room next to mine." Marc had already packed his things together. "Miles is grabbing more gear, as well."

Gear as in guns? She couldn't imagine what else they'd need.

Marc filled the small single-cup coffee dispenser with water. "Decaf, right?"

"Yes, please." She was ridiculously pleased he'd remembered she was avoiding caffeine because of the baby. When he handed her the cup, her fingers brushed his, sending a tingle of awareness up her arm. As nervous as she was, being with Marc gave her strength.

By the time they both had coffee, Mitch arrived with breakfast. Her stomach rumbled with hunger as the mouthwatering scents of French toast, maple syrup and bacon filled the room.

She was about to bow her head to pray, when Marc reached over to take her hand. She hung on, not ever wanting to let go.

"Dear Lord, we thank You for this food we are about to eat. We also ask that You keep us safe in Your care today as we seek justice. Amen."

"Amen," she whispered, touched by the fact that Marc was willing to pray with his brother standing there.

"Amen," Mitch added.

"Thank you, Marc," she said, reaching for a plastic fork. "That was nice."

His smile was lopsided. "You're going to be fine today," he said in a reassuring tone. "Between the three of us, we'll keep you safe."

"I believe you," she said.

They were halfway through breakfast when Miles arrived, carrying several heavy bags. She stared at them in confusion. What on earth did he bring? Surely, each of those bags wasn't full of weapons?

"Got body armor for all of us," Miles announced, dropping the bags on the bed. "Hope you have food left for me."

"Nope, we ate it all," Mitch said, popping a crispy slice of bacon into his mouth. "You'll have to get your own."

She frowned, glancing at the takeout container that still hadn't been opened. "Isn't this for Miles?"

Mitch groaned. "You weren't supposed to tell him yet," he said. "It would have been more fun to watch him get all riled up."

She flushed and shrugged, not used to the way siblings played jokes on each other.

"It's okay, Kari," Marc said with a quick wink. "They still think they're ten and twelve sometimes."

"Do not," Mitch huffed in protest. "We were in our teens when the practical jokes started."

Miles punched Mitch playfully in the arm before reaching over to pick up his food. "At least Kari is nice to me."

Her smile faded as a wave of intense longing hit hard. This camaraderie that existed between Marc and his brothers was something she'd always longed for. A sense of belonging that had eluded her since her mother passed away.

Her baby chose that moment to kick, as if reminding her that she wouldn't be alone for long. She placed a hand over her abdomen, enjoying the sensation.

When she lifted her head, she discovered three pairs of male eyes watching her intently. As if they'd never encountered a pregnant woman before.

Maybe they hadn't.

"I think this baby is going to be either a football player or a soccer player," she said, striving for a light tone. "He or she is pretty active these days."

Was it her imagination or was that a flash of longing she'd glimpsed in Marc's eyes? She told herself not to be foolish, but at the same time, she wanted it to be true.

"We're going to have you wear a bulletproof vest," he said, breaking the sudden silence. "If you're finished eating, I'd like you to try it on."

"Okay." She closed her empty container and rose to her feet.

Marc dug through the bag on the bed, then held out what looked to be a black vest. It looked huge and she stared at it doubtfully.

"I'm going to look silly wearing that over my clothes," she said.

"Actually, I'd like you to wear it under your sweater," Marc corrected. "Here's one of my T-shirts. Why don't you change into it, and we'll see how the vest fits?"

She did as he asked, going into the bathroom to change. Marc's T-shirt was soft and warm and smelled like him. She buried her nose in the fabric for a moment, filling her head with the comforting sandalwood scent, before stripping her baggy sweater off and pulling his shirt over her head.

It was long and a bit big, but she didn't mind. She carried her sweater out with her to join the brothers.

"Lift your arms up for me, please," Marc said, pulling the Velcro straps apart so that the vest was in two pieces. Working quickly, he managed to get the vest fitted around her torso. Her stomach pooched out a bit, but the vest was long enough to cover her down to her hips.

Marc stepped back, double-checking his handiwork. "That should work," he said mostly to himself. "Now we'll put the sweater on over it."

The sweater covered the vest, although with all the extra padding she knew she looked as if she'd gained forty pounds. Not that vanity was important.

"Looks good," Mitch said in agreement. "We should probably get going, since our plan is to arrive before everyone else."

Marc didn't say anything. He was still looking at her with such intensity she wondered if she looked worse than she thought.

"I'm ready, too," Miles added, pushing his empty breakfast container aside. "Marc? Are you all set?"

"Yeah, I'm good to go," he said in a deep husky voice. For a long moment she thought he might kiss her again, but then he turned toward his brothers. "We all need to suit up first, though."

Kari watched as all three of the Callahans pulled off their thick sweaters to put on their own vests. She was glad they'd be covered, too, and found herself hoping that all these precautions would prove unnecessary. She found it hard to believe anything would happen to her between now and eight thirty in the morning, when she was scheduled to be in the federal courthouse, ready to testify.

Please, Lord, give me the strength and courage to do this.

Her silent prayer helped keep her calm as the guys gathered everything together, obviously intending to check out of the motel rooms.

She felt another pang at knowing her time with Marc was coming to an end.

She'd miss him so much. His strength, his kindness, his protectiveness. She sucked in a harsh breath.

She cared about him. Far more than she should.

Twenty-five minutes later, Marc glanced at Kari, wondering what she was thinking. She'd been unusually quiet on the drive downtown. "There's the courthouse," he said, gesturing toward the right side of the truck. "It's pretty dark now because it's six thirty in the morning, but that's where you'll testify."

She nodded. "Looks impressive. Where's the entrance to the underground parking?"

"Mitch and Miles are heading there first, to make sure the coast is clear. They'll call me when it's safe to bring you down there."

"I see." She shifted in her seat. "I don't know how you guys get used to wearing this stuff. It's heavy."

He shrugged, deciding not to point out that wearing the safety gear was better than the alternative. "It's not so bad. You get used to it."

"Maybe you do," she said, lips slanting downward.

He scrubbed a hand over the back of his neck, wishing the niggling feeling in his gut would go away. When his phone rang, he started badly, proof that his nerves were on edge.

"Yeah?"

"It's clear, but there are more cars down here than we anticipated at this hour," Miles said.

The niggling sensation got worse. "Okay, we're on our way." He turned to face Kari. "Ready?"

"Absolutely," she said with what sounded like false cheerfulness.

Marc circled the block then approached a narrow entrance to the underground parking garage. The area was well lit, and he frowned when he saw what Mitch meant. Most of the parking spaces were empty, except for one or two older-model cars that looked like they might belong to the cleaning crew.

But over near the doorway that opened up to a stairwell, there were well over a dozen cars parked.

Two of the vehicles belonged to Miles and Mitch; they'd chosen spaces as close to the stairwell as possible.

Marc parked the truck between his brothers. "I don't like it," he said with a dark scowl. "What's with all the cars?"

"I don't know, but I agree it looks suspicious," Miles admitted. "We checked—they're all empty."

Marc drummed his fingers on the steering wheel. "What if they're rigged to blow? That kind of diversion would cause enough chaos that someone could get to Kari."

She let out a sound of distress and he hated the way she'd gone pale.

Miles and Mitch exchanged a long look. "We'll take a closer look," Mitch said.

"Maybe we should get a bomb-sniffing dog here," Marc suggested. "There's no way we can break into every vehicle in order to search them. Even if we tried, we might miss something."

"Good idea," Miles said. "I'll call in a few favors, see if I can get someone to come without going through official channels."

Marc glanced at his watch, hoping that the bomb-sniffing dog would get here before anyone else showed up. It was difficult to know who to trust, when he had no idea where the threat was coming from.

Kari shivered beside him and he turned in his seat to face her. "It will be okay. We're just being extra cautious."

"I know." Her voice was so quiet he could barely hear her. "I trust you."

He closed his eyes for a moment, thinking back to the witness he'd lost over a year ago. Joey Simmons had trusted him, too. A fact that hadn't worked out too well.

Not again, Lord. Please, not again...

Miles rapped sharply on his window, so he pushed the button to lower it. "A friend of mine, Connor Black, will be here soon with Duchess."

Marc assumed Duchess was the dog. "Great, thanks."

True to his word, Connor Black arrived in the parking structure fifteen minutes later. The black-haired guy slid out of the car, then opened the back passenger-side door to let out a large German shepherd. Duchess nimbly jumped down to the ground, then sat on her haunches beside Connor, waiting patiently as he attached a leash to her collar.

"Stay back while she's working," Connor instructed. Then he said something in a low tone to the dog and gestured to the parked cars.

Marc was impressed at how the dog worked methodically, sniffing around each car, then working her way down the row. She took her time, sometimes circling back to sniff at an area again before moving on.

The underground parking garage was completely quiet except for the sound of Duchess's nails clicking on the concrete. He could hear increased sounds of traffic from the street outside, and wasn't surprised when the first car entered the parking garage.

Using his rearview mirror, he tracked the vehicle as it wove through the parking spaces. The driver chose a spot a row or two behind them. When the driver slid out from behind the wheel, his attention was on the phone in his hand. When he pulled a briefcase out of the backseat, Marc pegged him for an attorney. The guy didn't seem to notice or care about Duchess, either, simply strode toward the doorway leading to the stairwell without looking back.

"No bombs," Miles said. "According to Connor and Duchess, the vehicles are clean."

"That's good news," Marc said in relief. "Maybe we've been worried over nothing."

Miles grunted, but didn't say anything more. Marc lifted a hand in thanks as Connor and Duchess drove away.

"It's seven o'clock," Mitch said, coming over to join them. "We're going to be seeing a lot of traffic coming in now, as people try to beat the rush. Of course, they'll only let attorneys and judges in this early. The general public isn't allowed in for another thirty minutes."

"I know." Marc tried to weigh the pros and cons of using his badge to get into the courtroom early. "What do you guys think? Should I take her in now and demand the bailiffs let us in?"

Miles let out a heavy sigh. "They'll likely call it in, which effectively announces that you're here with Kari, but maybe that doesn't really matter. After all, by the time they rush to get here, you'll already be safe inside."

"Unless the bailiff refuses to let them in," Mitch pointed out.

More cars were streaming into the structure and Marc didn't like it. "I'm willing to take the chance," he said. "I can probably call my boss if I have to." He hadn't talked to Evan White since the hurried phone call from the gas station on Friday, but surely his boss would understand.

"All right, let's go," Mitch agreed.

Marc climbed down from the truck and hurried over to assist Kari out. He knew her ability to move would be hampered by the heavy vest.

When she was steady on her feet, he shut the passenger-side door behind her. More and more cars streamed in, making him more nervous by the second. He tried to scan the people getting out of their respective vehicles to make sure none of them were members of the task force. He fully expected the task force to show up, but hoped they'd wait until he had Kari safe inside.

"Let's keep Kari between us," Marc said in a low voice.

His brothers nodded in agreement.

They walked toward the doorway leading to the stairwell. He tensed every time an attorney walked by. When they were halfway to the doorway, it opened abruptly and he saw Detective Steve Young standing there.

Marc stopped, his eyes narrowing with suspicion.

"Come on, I've made sure the stairwell is clear," Steve said. "Your boss requested extra protection."

Marc's hackles rose and he wished he'd personally talked to Evan White about the plan. He didn't trust anyone on the task force, and it sounded as if they all might be here.

Kari reached out and grasped his arm. "I recognize his voice," she whispered.

"What? How?"

"I heard him yelling at his wife. It was so bad I called the police."

Marc tightened his grip on Kari's arm. The stunned realization hit hard.

Detective Young was the leak!

"Too bad you recognized me Ms. Danville. I was hoping you wouldn't figure it out," Steve said.

Before Marc could say anything, Young pulled out his gun and pointed it at Kari.

"No!" Marc shouted, diving in front of Kari and taking the shot high in his left shoulder. Searing pain blinded him for several seconds before Miles shot back, sending Young flying backward into the stairwell with the force of the shot.

"Marc!" Kari screamed, dropping to her knees beside him. "What happened? Why is there so much blood? Did the bullet go through his vest?"

"Let me see," Mitch said, moving her gently aside. "Looks like the bullet hit him in the shoulder, just barely missing the vest. We'll need an ambulance."

Miles had gone to check Young, but then made his way back over to him.

"You promised," Marc said hoarsely, trying to ignore the burning pain. He reached out with his right hand to grab Mitch's arm. "Protect Kari. We don't know for sure that Young was working alone."

"I'm not leaving you. I'm calling for an ambulance," Kari said, pulling out her cell phone.

"Marc's right. We need to get you to safety," Mitch said. "Come on, let's go."

"No!" Kari shook off his grip. "We can't leave him!"

"Mike will be here soon. Don't worry."

Marc should have known his brothers would have had a backup plan, and he could hear Kari talking to the 911 operator as Mitch and Miles dragged her toward the stairwell. He groaned and lay back on the concrete floor, doing his best to stay alert.

His last conscious thought was to thank God that Kari hadn't been hit by Young's gunfire.

SEVENTEEN

Kari was so mad at Marc's brothers she could barely see straight. What was wrong with them? How could they leave him behind?

There was a gaping hole in her chest where her heart should be. And Kari knew that despite her stern lectures to herself, she'd once again foolishly fallen in love with the wrong man.

Not that Marc was anything like Vince, because he wasn't. But he'd closed himself off to love. And maybe even to having a family of his own.

The stark realization made it difficult for her to concentrate on what was going on around her. She was vaguely aware that Miles flashed his badge and spoke in undertones to the bailiff standing guard at the entrance to the courthouse. It took several minutes, but they were eventually allowed through.

"Mike will take care of him," Mitch said again, obviously sensing her distress. "Right now, we need you to testify so Marc doesn't suffer for nothing."

"There was so much blood," she whispered, as they made their way through the long hallways of the courthouse. "I hope the ambulance gets there in time."

"It will. Look, here we are," Miles said, opening the door with the name Judge Campbell written above it.

The hour was still early, but inside the courtroom she could see an attorney seated at the table on the right side, facing the judge. She didn't know if he was from the DA's office or was Jamison's attorney.

"ADA Welch?" Miles called. "I have information critical to your case. Detective Steve Young just took a shot at your witness. I returned fire, and unfortunately he's dead."

"What?" The attorney looked to be in his mid-forties, and immediately came over to where she was standing between Miles and Mitch. "When? Who else have you reported this to?"

"Just now and I haven't reported it to anyone else yet, because I need to keep Ms. Danville safe. FBI agent Marc Callahan dove in to protect her, taking the bullet in his shoulder."

The attorney swore under his breath. "I don't understand—what does Young have to do with this?"

"Good question," Miles said. "Why don't you

ask Jamison? He might be willing to talk if he knows Young is dead."

Welch was already pulling out his cell phone, no doubt contacting Jamison's lawyer. Kari turned toward Mitch. "Call your brother Mike. I need to know that Marc is getting the help he needs."

"The cell reception isn't great in here," Mitch warned.

"Just try," she urged.

"I'll be right back," ADA Welch said. "Jamison's attorney has agreed to talk."

Kari barely nodded, her gaze focused on Mitch.

"Mike? How is he?" There was a long pause before Mitch let out a sigh. "Okay, thanks. We'll meet you there."

"What happened?" she demanded when Mitch disconnected from the call.

"The ambulance is there and they're getting ready to take him to Trinity Medical Center." Mitch hesitated, then added, "He's lost a lot of blood. Apparently, they have a trauma surgeon standing by."

Tears pricked Kari's eyes and she reached out to grip Mitch's arm. She couldn't bear the thought of being away from Marc when he was injured. "I want to go with you when I'm finished testifying."

The two brothers exchanged a hesitant look. "We know Steve Young was involved," Miles said. "But unless Jamison talks, we won't know for sure that he was working alone. I'm sorry, but you still may need to go into witness protection."

"I need to know Marc will be all right," she said desperately. "Please, just take me there long enough to know he's all right."

"We'll see," Mitch said. But the way he avoided her gaze didn't give her much hope.

They sat in the courtroom for almost fifteen minutes before ADA Welch returned. "You were right. Jamison started talking. He admitted that he's related to Young. His mother is Young's sister. Jamison claims Young approached him about the bank robbery and wasn't talking because Young promised him he'd—" Welch made air quotes "—take care of everything."

"That figures," Mitch muttered.

"According to Jamison, Young went a little crazy when his wife divorced him and she took the house along with half his pension," ADA Welch continued. "He was extremely bitter because she'd ruined his chance at an early retirement."

"Is anyone else involved?" Miles asked.

"He gave us one other name in exchange for a lighter sentence. A guy by the name of Lee. Tomas Lee."

"He's dead," Kari interjected. "Isn't that what you told us, Miles?"

"Yeah, that's right," Miles agreed. "Lee's apartment had been ransacked and he was found dead in an alley not far from his place."

ADA Welch raised a brow. "So Young killed him? That's very interesting. I guess we won't need you to testify after all. Jamison admitted to doing the bank robberies and to shooting the bystander who tried to stop him. According to Jamison, the three of them were in it together. They even went out to get similar tattoos as they were putting their grand plans into place."

"I saw Lee's tattoo," Miles confirmed. "And you're right, Steve Young had one, too. It was covered, though, so I couldn't see much."

"I'm surprised Young tried to shoot you so close to the courthouse," ADA Welch said, frowning at Kari.

She swallowed hard, Marc's pale face seared into her memory. "I recognized his voice," she said hoarsely. "He used to live a few houses down from me, and I had to call the police one night when I heard yelling. They were fighting about money, and I clearly heard him swearing at his wife that she'd rue the day she took half of what he owned."

"And you think that was enough for him to try to kill you?" Welch asked.

She lifted her hands helplessly. "I can only assume he was worried that Marc would put two and two together, figuring out that he was the leak."

"We'll question Jamison some more to get more details about each of the robberies," Welch said. "But now that he's accepted a plea bargain, there's no need for you to testify, Ms. Danville. You're free to go."

The words reverberated in her mind. *Free to go!* She turned toward Mitch and Miles. "Take me to Trinity Medical Center."

"Okay," Miles agreed. "But only because I'm sure you're safe now."

"Amen to that," Mitch agreed.

Marc was in surgery when they arrived, so they sat together in the waiting room. Kari went into the bathroom to remove the bulky bullet-proof vest, relieved to have the additional weight off her shoulders.

After returning to the waiting room she handed the vest to Miles. "Thank you," she said in a low tone. "For everything." She felt bad that Miles had been forced to shoot Detective Young.

"No problem," Miles said, tossing the vest onto an empty chair. She could see both he and Mitch had already stripped their gear off, too.

The surgeon came out five minutes later. "Callahan?" he asked with a tired voice.

All four of them rose to their feet, although only Mike, Mitch and Miles were true Callahans. They didn't seem to mind when she tagged along.

"The bullet nicked an artery, so we had to give him several units of blood. But once the bleeding was controlled, he stabilized. He sustained a broken clavicle and the bullet punctured the upper lobe of his left lung, but thankfully the damage to his shoulder doesn't look too bad. He'll be in his room within the next hour or so."

"Thanks, doc," Miles said. The surgeon nodded, then left.

"Now that he's going to make it, I'll call to let Mom and Nan know." Mike pulled out his cell phone.

"They're out of town today, remember?" Miles said. "They mentioned at brunch yesterday that they were taking the train to Chicago for some last-minute Christmas shopping."

Mike stared at him. "I'll leave a message on Mom's cell phone," he said stubbornly. "You know she won't forgive me if I don't."

Kari sank into a seat, her knees feeling weak. The surgeon made it sound like Marc would be okay. She bowed her head and silently thanked God for keeping Marc safe.

Keeping them all safe.

The minutes ticked by with agonizing slowness. Finally, after nearly ninety minutes of waiting, a nurse came into the waiting room.

"Mr. Callahan is in room 320," she said. "You can visit two at a time, but remember he needs his rest."

Kari looked up at the three brothers. "I'll go in when you're finished," she offered.

Miles rolled his eyes. "Yeah, like Marc wants to see us," he said in a dry tone. "Come with me. You can stay with him. The three of us will take turns."

She nodded, even though she knew Miles was reading more into their relationship than what was really there. Just because she'd realized how much she cared for him didn't mean he felt the same way.

Besides, she shouldn't be listening to her heart. Hadn't she jumped into a relationship with Vince? But deep down, she knew she loved Marc. This was different than what she'd experienced with Vince. Marc had risked his life for her, over and over again.

He was a man worthy of her love. A man who deserved more than a woman like her, with a baby fathered by another man.

Marc was asleep when she and Miles entered the room. She crossed over to the bed and put her hand on Marc's arm, reassured by the way his chest rose and fell with each breath.

"It's over, Marc," she whispered. "Thank you for saving my life."

There was no sign that he'd heard her, but that was okay. She'd tell him again, once he woke up. Miles pulled the recliner over so that she could sit right next to his bed.

"Rest now," Miles told her in a gruff tone. "He'll be glad to see you when he wakes up."

She nodded, curling up in the recliner and reaching out so that her hand could rest lightly on his forearm. She'd wait, for as long as it took.

With a sense of urgency, Marc pushed through the pain, fighting to wake up. There was something important he had to do. But what?

He forced his eyelids open, blinking to bring the room into focus. The antiseptic smell was his first clue, along with the throbbing pain in his shoulder. The room came into focus. Hospital. Steve Young had tried to shoot Kari.

Kari!

He moved in the bed, intending to get up, only to suck in a harsh breath when the pain skyrocketed, making red spots dance in front of his eyes.

"Marc. You're awake."

He wasn't sure if the woman standing beside his bed was really Kari or something his pain-saturated mind conjured up. But then he felt the softness of her hands on his arms, as she gently pushed him down.

"Don't try to get up—you had surgery this morning. But the doctor says you're doing fine."

"You're here," he croaked, his voice raw and scratchy.

"Take a sip of water," she encouraged, holding out a cup with a straw.

The cool water felt amazing on his throat. He looked up at her. "Why aren't you with the US Marshals?"

"Because Jamison confessed. Young was the ringleader and Tomas Lee and Terrance Jamison were the ones who did the dirty work. When Jamison heard that Young was dead, he told the DA everything."

"Thank You, God," Marc said, feeling dizzy with relief.

"Rest now. Your brothers have been here—we're just waiting for your mother and grandmother to get back from Chicago."

He nodded, the sense of urgency fading away. Kari was here. She wasn't in danger anymore. She didn't have to leave.

He wouldn't have to live his life without her.

The next time he woke up, he felt marginally better. Glancing at the clock, he noticed it was two hours later, almost noon. He turned his head, his smile softening when he saw Kari curled in the recliner beside him.

She was so beautiful his heart ached. But beauty was only skin deep; what he loved the most was her kindness, her courage, her strength, her loyalty, her laughter.

Her faith.

It was too soon; they barely knew each other, but his heart didn't seem to realize that. He loved her. More than he'd thought possible.

He didn't want to wake her. As his gaze traveled over the room, he realized there were dozens of Mylar balloons surrounding his bed. Not just in the typical Christmas colors of red and green, although there were several of those, too, but also balloons of every color in the entire rainbow.

"What in the world?" he muttered.

"How are you feeling?" Kari asked, yawning sleepily as she unfolded herself from the chair.

"Better," he acknowledged. "What's with the balloons?"

She blushed and gave him an adorable smile. "I wanted you to wake up to lots of cheerful colors."

"They're nice, but not as pretty as you."

She blushed again, and then said, "Oh!"

"What is it?" He noticed she put her hand on her abdomen. "The baby?"

"Kicking again," she said softly.

"May I?"

She smiled, reached out and took his right hand, pressing it over the spot. "Can you feel it?"

The movements were gentle, fluttery, but definitely there. He was awestruck to share this intimate moment with her. "Amazing."

"Marc?" His mother's voice from the doorway caught him off guard. "How are you feeling?"

He tried not to squirm beneath his mother's questioning gaze. He was thirty years old, and hadn't done anything improper. But when Kari let his hand go, he knew she was probably mortified, too.

"I'm fine, Mother. You and Nan shouldn't have rushed home."

"Of course we should rush home," she chided him. She came over, gave him a hug and a kiss, then she looked at Kari. "Hello, my name is Margaret Callahan, Marc's mother. This is Kathleen Callahan, Marc's grandmother."

"Kari Ann Danville," Kari said, taking his mother's hand. "It's nice to meet you both. I was Marc's witness, and I'm sorry to tell you that he was shot protecting me."

He didn't like the way she was acting so nervous around his mother and grandmother, and tried to think of a way to defuse the situation.

"Actually, I was just leaving." Kari stepped away from the bedside. "See you later."

"Wait. Don't go," Marc said, his voice sharper than he intended. "Please, stay."

Kari looked indecisive, as if she wanted to be anywhere but here. Marc could tell by the expression on his mother's face that she was interested in what the true nature of their relationship was, but thankfully she didn't push it.

"Yes, Kari, please do stay. We were just going to grab a bite to eat. We didn't eat anything on the train." His mother turned toward him. "We'll see you in a few hours, okay?"

"Yeah, sure." Marc loved his mother and grandmother, but right now, he wanted some time alone with Kari.

After his family left, Kari sank into the chair and buried her face in her hands. "I'm sure they're wondering why a pregnant woman is here with you and who the father of the baby is."

"Kari, don't." He reached out and brushed her arm with his fingertips. "They won't judge you."

She lifted her head to look at him. "Of course they will. What mother wouldn't? They love you and they only want what's best for you."

"And what if I told you that you're what's best for me?" He hadn't intended to blurt it out quite so bluntly, but then again, finesse wasn't his thing. "You, Kari. And the baby you're carrying."

She sucked in an audible breath, looking stunned. "You—can't mean that."

"I do mean it. Being shot helps to put things in perspective. You were right to fill my room with color. I didn't even realize how dull and boring my world had become until I met you."

"Oh, Marc," she breathed. "You deserve so much more than a woman like me, who ended up pregnant by another man."

"I don't deserve someone as special as you," he corrected. "And your baby is a blessing from God. It doesn't matter to me who his father is, I still want to be there for you. For him."

A smile tugged at the corner of her mouth. "What if he's a she?"

"Then I hope she looks and acts just like her mother," he said somberly. "Beautiful inside and out."

She stared at him for a long moment. "I don't know what to say. We've only known each other a short time."

"I know. And I'm willing to give you all the time you need. But Kari?" He waited until she met his gaze. "I think I'm falling in love with you."

She moved closer to his bedside and took his

hand between both of hers. "Maybe that's just the pain medication talking."

He tried to hide the flash of annoyance, understanding that the words came from her own uncertainty. "It's not the pain medication. I know we haven't even gone out on a date yet, so I get where you're coming from. So let me ask you this—will you please join me and my family for church and brunch next Sunday?"

Her mouth dropped open. "With your entire family?"

"Yes. And I should warn you, that meeting the family isn't something to be taken lightly. None of us invite casual dates to Sunday service and brunch. But I'm asking you. Will you go with me?"

She didn't answer for so long he was afraid she was trying to figure out a way to let him down gently. Then she smiled and lifted his hand to her cheek.

"Yes, Marc. I'd love to join you and your family for service and brunch."

"I'm glad," he rasped.

"I guess it's only fair to warn you, that I think I'm falling in love with you, too."

His heart leaped in his chest. "Kari, I can't lift myself upright, so will you please come down here so I can kiss you?"

She laughed and bent over, covering his mouth

with hers. He cupped her head and held her close, until she broke away, struggling to breathe.

Their kiss had been too brief, but it held the promise of an amazing future.

EPILOGUE

Christmas Eve

Kari stared at her reflection in the bathroom mirror and tugged on the maternity dress she wore. She wished her bump weren't quite so noticeable, not that she was ashamed of her baby. Still, there was no mistaking her condition now.

She and Marc had spent every possible moment together these past three weeks. She'd attended every Sunday family gathering. She'd been humbled and honored to be welcomed by his family. His sister, Madison, in particular had pulled her aside last week and told her how glad she was that Kari had put the light back in Marc's eyes.

Now they'd be going to his mother's house for Christmas Eve dinner and no matter what Marc said, this was different.

Spending holidays together was something serious couples did.

She took a deep breath to steady her ragged nerves and then left the bathroom to join the fray. The minute she walked into the kitchen, Marc crossed over to her.

"Everything okay?" he asked, putting his arm around her shoulder and placing his hand protectively on her stomach. He'd been doing that a lot lately, and she couldn't deny how incredible it felt. Once she'd been worried about how well Marc would accept her baby, but she didn't have that fear anymore. He'd made it clear in so many different ways that he was in for the long haul.

"Of course," she strove for a light tone. "What can I do to help?"

"Nothing. There are too many cooks in this kitchen as it is," Maggie declared. "One more might tip us over the edge."

Maddy rolled her eyes at her mother's drama. "Relax, get off your feet. We'll be ready in about thirty minutes."

"Let's sit by the fire," Marc suggested.

Kari settled on the sofa and Marc took the seat right beside her. The Christmas tree was beautifully adorned with tiny twinkling white lights and gorgeous handmade ornaments. The logs in the fireplace cracked and popped. Kari wondered how she'd managed to be so fortunate to be here with the Callahan family.

"This is so nice," she murmured.

"You're right," Marc agreed huskily. "And I won't take my family for granted ever again."

She smiled, then gasped when he placed a tiny silver box in her lap.

"This is my Christmas gift to you," he said in a low voice. When she simply stared at it, he gave her a little nudge. "Go ahead, open it."

She ripped the box open, like a two-year-old expecting her favorite toy. Her chest swelled when she saw the small black velvet jewelry case.

Inside was a beautiful sapphire ring surrounded by small diamonds.

"Oh, Marc," she said breathlessly. "It's stunning."

"You like colors, so I went with a gemstone rather than a center diamond."

"I'm glad. It's too much, but I love it."

"Kari, will you marry me?" Marc lifted out the ring and slid it onto the fourth finger of her left hand. "I know it's fast, but I think we should be married before our baby is born, don't you?"

She stared up at him in shocked surprise, then curled into his arms. "Yes, Marc. Yes, I'll marry you."

He bent his head, covering her mouth with his. "I love you," he murmured. Then he dipped his head to press a kiss on her belly. "And I love this little guy, too."

Kari laughed and shook her head. "We both love you, too. And you better stop calling her a him, or she's going to be confused once she's born."

"Well? Did she say yes?"

Kari glanced over her shoulder to see the entire Callahan clan hovering in the doorway, waiting expectantly. She blushed and nodded.

"Welcome to our family," Maggie said, her eyes bright with tears.

"Thank you," Kari managed before her vision clouded, as well.

"Can't you give me five more minutes," Marc groused. "I'd like to kiss my fiancée in private."

There was some giggling and groaning as they returned to the kitchen.

When his mouth captured hers, Kari couldn't think of a better Christmas gift.

New beginnings with a new family.

* * * * *

Dear Reader,

I'm so excited to introduce the first book in my Callahan Confidential series. The Callahan family has a legacy of choosing careers that support the community, but their jobs also put them in danger. I always enjoy writing Christmas stories so it's fitting that the first book in my Callahan series is a holiday story.

Shielding His Christmas Witness introduces you to serious and somber FBI agent Marc Callahan. Marc's first marriage was on the rocks before his wife died, and he's shut himself off from his family and his faith as a result of her death. When Marc discovers that his safe house has been compromised, putting his pregnant witness, Kari Danville, in danger, he's determined to do whatever is necessary to protect her. He'll even risk his life, but will he expose his heart?

I hope you enjoy Marc and Kari's story. I'm hard at work on the next book in the series featuring Miles Callahan. I enjoy hearing from my readers. If you're interested in dropping me a brief note, or in signing up for my newsletter, please

visit my website at www.laurascottbooks.com.
I'm also on Facebook at Laura Scott Books Author
and on Twitter @Laurascottbooks.

Yours in faith,
Laura Scott